CLASS ACTION

By **Steven B. Frank**

HOUGHTON MIFFLIN HARCOURT
BOSTON NEW YORK

Copyright © 2018 by Steven B. Frank

All rights reserved. For information about permission to reproduce selections from this
book, write to trade.permissions@hmhco.com or to Permissions, Houghton Mifflin
Harcourt Publishing Company, 3 Park Avenue, 19th Floor, New York, New York 10016.

hmhbooks.com

The text was set in Perrywood MT Std.
Map of the National Mall and Memorial Parks on pp. 160–61
courtesy of the National Parks Service.

The Library of Congress has cataloged the hardcover edition as follows:
Names: Frank, Steven, 1963– author.
Title: Class action / by Steven B. Frank.
Description: Boston ; New York : Houghton Mifflin Harcourt, [2018]
Summary: With the help of his older sister, his three best friends, and his elderly
neighbor, sixth-grader Sam Warren brings a class action suit against the
Los Angeles School Board, arguing that homework is unconstitutional,
and his case goes all the way to the Supreme Court.
Identifiers: LCCN 2017014151
Subjects: | CYAC: Legal stories. | Homework—Fiction.
Classification: LCC PZ7.1.F746 Cl 2018 | DDC [Fic]—dc23
LC record available at https://lccn.loc.gov/2017014151

ISBN: 978-1-328-79920-3 hardcover
ISBN: 978-0-358-11802-2 paperback

Printed in the United States of America
DOC 10 9 8 7 6 5 4 3 2 1
4500760932

FOR MY STUDENTS, WHOSE HOMES I MAY HAVE UNLAWFULLY ENTERED OVER THE YEARS.

Aaron Kaplan
Adam Abergel
Adam Cumurcu
Adam Driscoll
Adam Hahn-Edel
Adam Riancho
Adam Stockhoff
Adele Marquez-Luttringer
Adèle Roskin
Adia Chapman
Adnan Khoja
Adrien Forney
Adrien Girard
Adrien Jaijar
Adrien-Julien Vaatete
Ahmed Tar
Aidan Koslu
Aidan Milner
Aina Hashimoto
Aïsha Bortolotti
Alain Triquenaux
Alan Tambelini
Alanna Lesueur
Alec Boulbain
Aleena Antonino
Alejandra Razo

Alejandro Quintana
Alessandra Chaves
Alessandra Vietina
Alessandro Harabin
Alessandro Moroder
Alexa Gozlan
Alexa Mansour
Alexander Auge-Opman
Alexander Fox-Walker
Alexander Franchi
Alexander Friedman
Alexander Groothaert
Alexander Ingersoll
Alexander Miora
Alexander Pierre
Alexander Rasgon
Alexander Shirokow-
    Louden
Alexander Sissoko
Alexander Von Banck
Alexandra Bonnet
Alexandra Colombo
Alexandra Connor
Alexandra Haynes
Alexandra Ivie
Alexandra Jackson

Alexandra Kabbaz-Szabo
Alexandra Kao
Alexandra Nissani
Alexandra Rivier
Alexandra Wisner
Alexandre Anselme
Alexandre Derytcz
Alexandre Ertaud
Alexandre Forney
Alexandre Miaule
Alexandre Moritz
Alexandre Ragson
Alexandre Senacq
Alexandre Vigier
Alexandria Jackson
Alexandrine Bonaparte
Alexia Britsch
Alexia Caramitsos
Alexia Nahai
Alexia Saleh
Alexie Rubin
Alexis Boris
Alexis Heruth
Alexis Rowley
Alexis Whitman Heruth
Alice Hutin

Alice Velle
Alicia Lacock
Aliona Pitchkar
Alirayan Helmi
Alireza Imani
Alison Bensimon
Alistair Nash
Alix Braud
Alizé Jean
Allana Baker
Allegra Kuklowski
Allegra Sotudeh
Allison Dixon
Alona Zaray-Mizrahi
Amadea Choplin
Amalie Kaerskov
Amanda Beker
Amanda Coad
Amanda Newman
Amanda Penichet
Amaury Lannes
Amber Collins
Amber Pourdihimi
Amber Tar
Amber Vaatete
Ambre Campbell
Ambre Nash
Amelia Matteson
Amélie Bushong
Amélie Butler
Amélie Demey
Amélie Desmarchelier
Amélie Lavalée
Amir Amirsaleh
Amir Ensani
Amir Hadidi
Amissa Bongo-Ondimba
Amy Chabassier

Amy Enayati
Ana-Maria Moldovan
Anabel Cormier
Anaelle Chwat
Anaïs Tunzini
André Kludjian
André Vo
Andrea Leal
Andrea Nevil
Andrea Perez-Bertolotto
Andreas Homer-Bezamat
Andrew Borin
Andrew Elosseini
Andrew Hamlin
Andrew Kierszenbaum
Andrew Schwanke
Andrew Senkfor
Andy Kumar
Angela Adler
Angele Beasse
Angele Fernandez
Angelica Kechichian
Angelina Cosci
Angélique Atencio
Angélique Bosc
Angie Bagheri
Ann Wands
Ann-Jacqueline Beish
Anna Gobin
Anna Parker
Anna Treyson
Annalyse Atlan
Anne-Sophie Frossard
Anne-Sophie Leary
Anne-Victoria Delolmo
Annie Yamaguchi
Annie-Marie Franko
Annik Merckx

Anouk Jouffret
Ansel Faraj
Anthany Khaiat
Anthony Bayac
Anthony Bell
Anthony Rubin
Antoine Gobin
Antoine Leroux
Antoine Megevand
Antoine Van Lier
Antonia White
Antonin Giraud
Ari Warnaar
Ariane Aumont
Arianne Atlan
Arianne Nash
Arielle Pytka
Arielle Soussan
Arion Amanuel
Arthur Belais
Arthur Rousselin
Arya Emami
Arya Malek
Arya Zanganeh
Aryel Andrieu
Ashcon Hassanpour
Asher Cohen
Ashlen Mezrahi
Ashley Greene
Ashley Hinshaw
Ashley Sloan
Ashley St.-Amand
Asia Chow
Astrid Burgess
Athena Mansour
Athena Simeran
Audrey Choi
Audrey Michaels

August Massonat

Augustin Jouslin de Noray

Augustin Redon

Aurelia Rappaport

Aurélie Magnier

Austin Hines

Austin Kabbaz-Szabo

Ava Atlan

Ava Harvey

Ava Scaturro

Axel Van den Esch de Jessé

Ayden Mavany

Azita Mireshghi

Babak Abrishamchian

Barrett Ahn

Barthelemi Touffu

Basil Katz

Basile Pelletier

Beau Barnett

Behin Behrozi

Benjamin Athlan

Benjamin Bismuth

Benjamin Brizzi

Benjamin Lopategui

Benjamin Miora

Benjamin Montesinos

Benjamin Schmitt

Benjamin Simeran

Bennette-Kate Ross

Bianca McGuire

Bianca Saint-Cricq

Bita Tanavoli

Blair Di Giacomo

Blanche Powell

Blue Tencanera

Boris Ivshin

Borja Ballarin

Bosco Gonzalez-Chudoba

Brady Keith

Bram Kornfeld

Brandon Martin

Brandon Sheer

Brandon Takkieddine

Braxton Carr

Brennan Balsan

Brent Wisner

Brian Lucier

Brianna d'Estrie

Brigitte Campbell

Brigitte Perez

Brittany Craigo

Brittany Derrien

Brittany Forge

Bruno Vinogradoff

Bryan Chamchoum

Bryan Nakagawa

Bryce Bannatyne

Bryce Ferguson

Buck Haddix

Caitlin Lalezari

Caleb Solomon

Calix Boldt

Calvin Atlan

Camelia Hssaine

Cameron Azia

Cameron Czerny

Camille Barker

Camille Ceugniet

Camille Everaert

Camille Gallardo-Laffitte

Camille Giraud

Camille Lordet

Camille Wormser

Carla Brizzi

Carla Bueono

Carmen Anton

Caroline Bertrand

Caroline Frauman

Caroline Gluck

Caroline Hartog

Caroline Levin

Caroline Werlin

Carolyn Smith

Cassandre Garnier

Cassiel Massonat

Catalina Rojter

Catherine Lee

Catherine Wu

Cayden Campbell

Cayla Minaiy

Cédric Vallée

Céline Allaverdian

Celine Azia

Celine Bezamat

Celine Kabaker

Celine Kuklowsky

Chamsi Hssaine

Chance Combs

Chanel Boisson

Chanelle Nibbelink

Charlee Washington

Charles Bertranou

Charles Frauman

Charles Osawa

Charles Ribeyre

Charlotte Ceugniet

Charlotte Coplon

Charlotte Del

Charlotte Everaert

Charlotte Kierszenbaum

Charlotte Le Caignec

Charlotte Leger

Charlotte Noël

Charmaine Midler

Chaya Schapiro

Chayanne Rigaud

Cheyenn Chretien

Chiara Conti

Chiara Vietina

Chloé Aubert

Chloé Bartoli

Chloé Bismuth

Chloé Dumortier

Chloé Franchi

Chloe Ginsburg

Chloé Lafferty

Christa Pedersen

Christian Munoz-Walmsley

Christian Torchon

Christine Ciuca

Christine Doublet

Christine Hovanessian

Christopher Ching

Christopher Cole

Christopher Fervel

Christopher Gibson

Christopher Hooks

Christopher Leger

Claire Dinhut

Claire Nordin

Clara De Goldsmith

Clara Ly

Clara Mokri

Clara Nicolas

Clara Warnaar

Clare Larsen

Clarisse Forestier

Clarisse Wiedem

Clay Dumas

Clémence du Cleuzio

Clémence Ollivier

Clémentine Todorov

Clovis Schlumberger

Clovis Weisbart

Cole Hattler

Colette Gilbert

Colombine Verciel

Colombine Zamponi

Constance Delahousse

Constantin Sauvage

Constantin Savvides

Contessa Popeil

Corentin Roux

Cornelius Robbins

Courtney Sherman

Curtis Crowe

Cylia Chasman

Cyril Rocoffort

Cyril St.-Girons

Cyrille Ateba

Cyrus Amin

Daisy-Tiare Lintilhac

Dana Nissim

Danica Kreculj

Daniel Ben-Naiem

Daniel Cheng

Daniel de Polignac

Daniel Lee

Daniel Palmieri

Daniel Samson-Iwata

Daniel Siegwart

Daniella Mezrahi

Danielle Gilbert

Danielle Groper

Danielle Safady

Dante Ray

Daphné Hacquard

Daphne Moss

Darien Jose

Darina Scotti

Dario Pucci

Darius Leoncavallo

Davery Joso

David Berdakin

David Cambay

David Charrin

David Nealy

David Noble

David Zaghdoudi-Allan

David Zaray-Mizrahi

Deen Tar

Delphine Duchemin-
Harvard

Deniz Senkan

Derek Blumenfield

Derek Stewart

Devon Lee

Dhamin Kerstens

Diana Tsvitichvili

Dianah Oh

Didier Guellai

Diego Berdakin

Diego Ruiz

Dominique Borno

Dominique Sirgy

Dominique Tordjmann

Dominique-Michelle
Duchemin

Dorian Bey

Dorian Le Tellier
Guérineau

Dustin Benichou

Dustin Song

Edouard Chaltiel

Edward Cutter

Eileen Deng
El Mamoune Cherkaoui
Elango Kumaran
Eleni Tadross-Marks
Eléonore Lund-Simon
Eleri Cousins
Eliana Fuller
Elijah Moses
Elijah Nozaïque-
    Kratchman
Eliona Gabler
Elisa Gourlet
Elisabeth Berard Godbout
Elisabeth Rollin
Elise Le Cam
Elissa Shanshan Heh
Elita Kahen
Eliza Cuny-Valdetaro
Elizabeth Benichou
Elizabeth Froehlig
Elizabeth Langlois
Elizabeth Martinkovic
Elizabeth Moore
Ella Fletcher
Ella Larsen
Elodie Blumberg
Eloise Kabbaz-Szabo
Eloise Ngo
Elon Wertman
Elsa Hanson
Emilie Maniquis
Emilie Sherman
Emily Arlen
Emily Broutian
Emily Yang
Emma Ferguson
Emma Garnier-Beausoleil

Emma Luppi
Emma Meigneux
Emma Nylund
Emma Walther
Emma Wollman
Emmanuel Ghil
Emmanuelle Roumain-
    Yang
Emmanuelle Weisbach
Eric Noble
Eric Penichet
Erica Bagby
Erica Fyhrie
Erica Huron
Erik Merckx
Erik Schmidt
Erika Wallman
Erika Wiese
Erin Buckelew
Erin Foley
Estelle Aflalo
Estelle Allouche
Ethan Bonnan
Etienne Leroux
Etienne Tremblay
Eugénie Lund-Simon
Eva Gabor Fourcade
Eva Hartge
Evelyn Hammid
Eytan Boon
Fabian Salazar
Fabien Roland
Fabio Angulo
Farah Issa
Faten Sayed
Feben Alula
Federica Bonetti

Felix Lutterbeck
Felyjos Duchemin
Feras Barakat
Fernando Sotomayor
Fig Camille Abner
Firuz Yumul
Florentino Sotomayor
Francesca Shay
Francine Yansané
Francis Gon-Gibbs
Francois Jarrault
François Miaule
Frank Pellegrino
Frankie Belle Stark
Frankie Pugliese
Frédéric Brizzi
Frédéric Petit
Frederick Duncan
Gabi Rozavski
Gabriel Borsuk
Gabriel Lister
Gabriel Palmieri ·
Gabriel Rousseau
Gabriel Vergel de Dios
Gabriela Hirschler
Gabriela Perez-Bertolotto
Gabriell Choate
Gabriella Fern
Gabriella Hirschler
Gabriella Onggara
Gabrielle Butler
Gabrielle Levesque
Gael Petrina
Gaia Curatolo
Gaia Khatchadourian
Garrett Galati
Gauillaume Léger

Gelen Hinshaw

Geneva Carter

George Cornejo

George Osawa

Georgi Zlenko

Georgianna Chang

Gérard Khatchadourian

Giancarlo Azzarelli

Gianna Carelli

Gigi Baybrooks

Gigi Nibbelink

Gina Oh

Ginger Taurek

Giordono Bonoro-Groome

Giulia Nunnari

Golriz Moezzi

Grace Rocoffort de
Vinnière

Grant Palmer

Grégoire Vaz

Gregory Valentin

Griffen Thorne

Griffin Gluck

Guillaume Goulin

Guillaume Le Balle

Guillermina Sola

Gunter Sissoko

Gus Ahn

Hana Kidaka

Hana Navab

Hanna Ghadessi

Hanna Welter

Hannah Fitzgerald

Hannah Kierszenbaum

Hannah Welter

Henry Coquillard

Henry Crawford

Henry Hunter-Hall

Henry Putnam

Henry Roskin

Heyden Silberman

Hiram Lannes

Hisham Sebai

Holly Hessamian

Holly Wertman

Hyun Lee

Ian Ehrlich

Ilana Kratchman

Ilona Slama

Ilya Garachine

Ilyes Aouragh

Iman Burks

In-Ho Hwang

India-Rose Walker-Folliard

Inès Falliex

Isaac Mimoun

Isabel Schlueter

Isabella De Falco

Isabella Goetschel

Isabella Goodson

Isabella Haddad

Isabella Mandich

Isabella Ranzlov

Isaure Sander

Island Gabler

Ivy Maurice

Izya Cibert-Lebtahi

Jack Dubois

Jack Phelan

Jack Tucker

Jacob Larimer

Jacqueline Shay

Jacqueline Vogel

Jade De Jaham

Jade Gauriat

Jade Smet

Jaesang Noh

James De Gallegos

James Goodman

Jamie Stern

Jan Frybes

Jana Barakat

Janan Aouragh

Jane Tanimura

Jane Weitz

Janna Freedman

Jasmine Brown

Jasmine Wells

Jason Kuyper

Jay Jacob

Jazz Johnson

Jean Christophe Worth

Jean-Alexandre Fervel

Jean-Charles Massonat

Jean-Guillaume Caillaud

Jean-Marc Murray

Jean-Philippe Ateba

Jean-Philippe Riol

Jean-Pierre Richard

Jean-Yves Trouveroy

Jeandre Diaz

Jeffrey Goldenberg

Jemina Auge

Jennifer Nibbelink

Jennifer Sherwood

Jennifer Tartavull

Jensen Fitzgerald

Jeremy Altervain

Jeremy Kaufman

Jeremy Shawaf

Jeremy Yon

Jerico Walker-Roberts	Josephine Clark	Kaede Daley
Jérôme Maurin	Joséphine Whittaker	Kaiya Gales
Jesse Axel de Van Den Esch	Joshua Cedicci	Kamilla Aouragh
Jesse Richards	Joso Darien	Karl Marzec
Jessica Kao	Jude Stephenson	Kate Brillstein
Jessica Sabbah	Judith No	Katelyn Artiga
Jeyraan Yazdani	Jules Villaret	Katherine Ingersoll
Jimena Gonzalez	Julia Mazur	Katherine Ireland
Jivan Girodet	Julia Petrus-Verstraeten	Katherine Lemoine
Jo-Alexander Baes	Julian Borda	Kathryn Geller
John Cornet	Julian Brannon	Katia Bassal
John Smith	Julian Craig	Katie Tower
John-Alexandre Goodman	Julian Vergel de Dios	Kaya Ezidore
John-Paul Hreha	Julie Coulin	Kayla Foster
Joie Bacote-Williams	Julie Gaudru	Keilye Rivera
Joie Walls	Julie Le Caignec	Keivan Darius Golchini
Jolie Feld	Julien Borno	Kelly Royère
Jonah Gozlan	Julien Brock	Kelsey Jacquard
Jonas Bensimon	Julien de Goldsmith	Kelsey Read
Jonathan Ameli	Julien Jean	Kenza Schnur
Jonathan Dekhtyar	Julien Levesque	Kevin Greene
Jonathan Elosseini	Julien Yansané	Kevin Henson
Jonathan Goodman	Juliette Cornet	Khadijah Mavany
Jonathan Hockley	Juliette Leclerc	Khai Fujita
Jonathan Saleh	Juliette Pierre	Kilee Delaney
Jonathan Saltzman	Juliette Riancho	Kim Buisson
Jonathan Weisberg	Juliette Schmidli	Kimberley Dahl
Jonathan Zinberg	Justice Johnson	Kimberley Mark
Jordan Hickey	Justin Choi	Kimberly Goodman
Jordan Miller	Justin Kuyper	Kristian Henson
Jordan Sotudeh	Justin Lannoy	Kristian Stark
Jordan White	Justin Marchand	Kristin Joseph
Jordyn Garcia Carey	Justin Miyahira	Kyle Luethge-Stern
Joseph Abergel	Justine Allouch-Chantepie	Laetitia de Parisot
Joseph Bodner	Justine Cornet	Laetitia Ribeyre
Joseph Girton	Justine Mathieu	Laila Fletcher
Joseph Perrette-Lazard	Justine Runel	Lailee Mavadat

Lama Taher
Lara Bond
Lara Laing
Laura Wright
Laure Gérard
Laure Le Pendeven
Laure-Anne Ventouras
Laurel Fisher
Lauren Ifergan
Lauren Ravon
Lauren Tarnoff
Laurence Cormier
Laurent Alberti
Laurent Laughlin
Laurianne Magnier
Lawrence Cicuca
Léa Boulbain
Léa Dumortier
Léa Hervas
Lea Spicker
Lea Yamaguchi
Leah Hands
Leah Khalili
Léana Borsuk
Leanne Gozlan
Leila Etessami-Decker
Leila Hinshaw
Leland Farmer
Lenny Delitz
Leo Alberti
Leo Fradet
Léo Major
Léo Thomasson
Léon Bruel Benguigui
Liam Edwards
Liam Garnier
Liana Wertman

Liberty Johnson
Lilah Khoja
Liliana Chomsky
Lilie Kulber
Lillia Parsa
Lillie Laing
Lilliebelle Hannes
Lilou Peyrache
Lily Gevorkian
Lily Nicksay
Lina Boukhateb
Lina Yildiz
Lindsey Le Plae
Linus Stroetzel
Lisa Bigot
Lisa Royère
Lisa Wiener
Lola Herry
Lorenzo Turci
Lorig Koujakian
Lorraine Forestier
Lorraine Lannes
Lou Lou Safran
Lou-Andréa Goss
Lou-Anne Mathieu
Louie Kulber
Louis Nissani
Louis Petauton
Louise Powell
Loup Marquez-Luttringer
Luana Vinogradoff
Luca Aiche
Luca Boldrini
Lucas Burgess
Lucca Fletcher
Lucia Ponti
Lucia Ruiz-Herberg

Lucia Stroetzel
Lucian Bonaparte-Wyse
Lucie Combredet
Lucius Cary
Luis Jaggy
Luken McGuire
Lulla Dawood
Luna Souchard
Lysandre Judd
MacKenzie Munro
Madeleine Holtz
Madison Burnett
Madison Young-McColgan
Maëlys Ezidore
Maëylis Lescauville-
    Tournissac
Magali Bey
Magali Duque
Magali Duque
Mahdouneh Imani
Maissa Makdisi
Maissa Makdisi
Maite Laurient
Maïté Laurient
Makaylo Van Peebles
Maleen Smith
Mamadou-Lamine N'Diaye
Mana Nagaï
Manaka Nagai
Manon De Solstice
Manon de Solstice Antonio
Mara McKevitt
Maram Nazer
Marc Fiorentino
Marc Nicolas
Marcela Leal
Marcos Morinigo

Margaux Darius	Matthew Alberti	Michael Cheng
Margaux Machat	Matthew Alschuler	Michael Dalson
Margot Jaggy	Matthew Simanian	Michael Ghebrial
Marguerite Vericel	Maunu Riipinen	Michael Hein
Marie Ballester	Maureen Palos	Michael Hessamian
Marie Bobin	Maurice Pessah	Michael Koechlin
Marie Boubon	Maurice Simanian	Michael Parsa
Marie Bougeard	Max Kofsky	Michael Perez
Marie de Sarthe	Max Lutterbeck	Michael Smith
Marie de Sousa	Max Schlesinger	Michael Talei
Marie-Lou Bartoli	Maxence Guérout	Michaela Maxwell
Marie-Louise Khondji	Maxim Sabadash	Mielle Mann
Marielle Lerner	Maxime Bigot	Mihran Konanyan
Marin Decoux	Maxime Isautier	Mila Horowitz
Marin Rousselin	Maxime La Balle	Mila Scheinberg
Marion Joffre	Maximilian Brambila	Milad Hajian
Marisol Macias	Maximilian Licona	Milan Côté Dréan
Marissa Bray	Maximiliano Rioja	Milan Matthew-Bryant
Marissa Hartwick	Maximilien Boutry	Milann Murray
Marissa Hattler	Maximillian Tinglof	Milena Krstic
Mark Solvason	Maxine Hoesdorf-Rosen	Mirabel Rouze
Marlen Zhornitsky	Maxwell Green	Mireille Owens
Marlowe Barnett	Megan Friend	Mirella Ghil
Martin Hendleman	Megan Hurley	Misha Louy
Martin Janneau-Houllier	Mehammed Mack	Misha-Arielle Cade
Martin Seifrid	Melanee Shale	Miuccia Judd
Mary Elizabeth Arlen	Melania Horowitz	Mizan Khasay
Mary Reid	Melanie Wiener	Monica Moldovan
Mathew Greene	Melissa Belloncle	Montana Murray
Mathew O'Neill	Melusine Maury	Morgan Golding
Mathieu Le Cam	Melvier Besnoin	Morgan Orwitz
Mathieu Wiener	Meredith Berk	Morgan Stewart
Mathilde Balland	Mia Louise Ray	Morgana Van Peebles
Matilda Criel	Micael Thiodet	Morgane Caen
Matisse Guillen	Micaela Arakelyan	Morgane de Place
Matisse Senkfor	Michael Bitton	Morgane Tresorier
Matteo Ugolini	Michael Brink	Morgane Worth

Morganna Van Peebles
Muhamed Mustafa
    Kothawala
Muhamed Reza Kothawala
Muhammad Tar
Muna Shamee
Naaz Amirsadeghi
Nadege Zaghdoudi -Allan
Nadia Rawjee
Nadine Peltier
Najah Sumpter-Diop
Najara Vanginaux
Nanar Astourian
Naomi Daneshgar
Naomi Larsen
Natalia Quintana
Natalie Pasallar
Natasha Guez
Natasha Hands
Natasha Heyman
Natasha Rossi
Natasha Zaidman
Nathalie Bray
Nathalie de Laguarique
Nathalie Demirdjian
Nathalie Didier
Nathalie Hendleman
Nathalie Van Helden
Nathalie Vorgeack
Nathan Benson
Nathan Chwat
Nathan Griot
Nathan Soussi
Nathaniel Del
Nathaniel Lalo
Nazanin Behzadpour
Nazgole Hamidi-Hashemi

Ned Moshay
Negar Shekarchi
Nicchi Battaglino
Nicholas Alschuler
Nicholas Barnett
Nicholas Callas
Nicholas Guez
Nicholas Maurin
Nicholas Pheffer
Nicholas Vigier
Nicholas Wasil
Nickie Toulouee
Nicolaï Alexander
Nicolas Beylier
Nicolas Duchemin-Harvard
Nicolas Guez
Nicolas Madzar
Nicolas Mak-Wasek
Nicolas Megevand
Nicolas Muraglia
Nicolas Rojter
Nicole Brik
Nicole Hopper
Nicole Liuzzi
Nicole Perez-Bertolotto
Nina Enayati
Nina Grangeon-Gomez
Nina Sutre
Nissa Merckx
Noah Solomon
Noor Afshar
Noor De Falco
Nour Issa
Océane Boisson
Olan Moon White
Oleg Khokhov
Oliver Doublet

Oliver Maclean
Oliver Nassiri
Oliver Putnam
Olivia Baes
Olivia Benchamou
Olivia Meadows
Olivia Sabbah
Olivier Berson
Olivier Curial de
    Brevannes
Olivier Morovati
Olivier Velde
Oluayanfe Idewu
Olympia Boris
Olympio Naufel
Omar Jurdi
Omar Spahi
Omid Moezzi
Oona Koslu
Oriana Gozlan
Oriana Isaacson
Ornella Esteras
Pablo Garms
Paloma Le Friant
Paola Kim
Paris Gingold
Pascal Title
Pascale Williams
Patric Lopez
Patrick Barnett
Patrick Ventouras
Paul Doulatshahi
Paul Keller
Paul Langlois
Paul Leclerc
Paul-Antoine Leloup
Paula Rollins

Paule Velle	Rachel Gidouin	Romy McGuire
Pauline Horwits	Rachel Mendoza	Ronan Delpech
Pearl Engler	Rafael Fortin	Rosie Clarkson
Pearse Matteson	Raimy Sakurada	Roxana Marten
Penelope Boutry	Ramin Taheri	Roxane Chabassier
Penelope Figueroa	Ranya Stover	Roxane Zargham
Penelope Liot	Raphael Amar	Roxanna Abrishamchian
Persia Phillips	Raphael Daneshgar	Roxanna Marten
Peter Karpushin	Rayhane Sanders	Royce Rowley
Peter Lai	Rebecca Johnson	Ruben Lalo
Peter Pettus	Rebecca Sharp	Ruby Love
Philip Mogil	Rémi Fletcher	Russel Nibbelink
Philip O'Neil	Rémi Nemeroff	Ryan Muraglia
Philip Shen	Rémy Balembois	Ryan Van Sant
Philippe de Sablet	Rémy Ertaud	Ryusuke Omiya
Philippe Welter	Rémy Tordjmann	Sabina Brink
Philippine Demesteere	Renalde Jett	Sabrina Kothwala
Philippine Sander	Renaud Cartron	Sacha Carotenuto
Phoebe Balson	Richard Kim	Sacha Pytka
Piero Karageozo	Riley Capton	Saffron Rose
Pierre Bougeard	Robbie Duncan	Sahel Fattahi
Pierre Derycz	Robert Arlen	Salar Tinossh
Pierre Dessertenne	Robert Behn	Salma Durra
Pierre Guillaud	Robert Crawford	Sam Iravani
Pierre Haijar	Robert Lazar	Sam Keyvan
Pierre Leger	Robert Sobieski	Sam Mehrizi
Pierre Perrin-Peltier	Robin Nicolas	Samantha McKenzie
Pierre Real	Rocio Macias	Samantha Reilly
Pierre Schlumberger	Rod Rezvani	Samantha Scheurer
Pierre Shamee	Roderick Besnoin	Samantha Seneviratne
Pierre-Alexis Devèze	Rodolphe Le Feuvre	Samara Roman-Holba
Pollyanna Clarkson	Roger Van Helden	Samir Ghazal
Pouya Yousef	Romain Lagree	Samir Makdisi
Quitterie Chassepot	Romain Leon	Samiya Sayed
Rachael Hune	Romain Soulies	Samuel Ulrich
Rachael Rebujio	Roman Usher	Sandra Bine-Dutray
Rachel Archer	Romano Barsioli	Sara Andreas

Sara Bodle

Sara de Falco

Sara Jour

Sara Khattab

Sara Tamers

Sarah Dumont

Sarah Enayati

Sarah Gianchandani

Sarah Gruman

Sarah Jenks

Sarah Le Cam

Sarah Maniquis

Sarah Monroe Aranzazu

Sarah Patterson

Sarvenaz Sara Helmi

Sasha Barrese

Sasha Gharibian

Sasha Podell

Sasha Pojzman

Sasha Radovanovic

Satya Amin

Sayeh Fattahi

Scarlett Gilreath

Scott Lassan

Sean Kennedy

Sean Stillman

Seana Moon White

Sebastian Borda

Sebastian Monoz-Walmsley

Sebastian Talib

Sebastien Balembois

Sebastien Burgess

Sébastien Rouman-Zala

Selma Khattab

Sephen Scheinberg

Serena de Mouroux-Phelan

Serene Obagi

Sergey Derevianko

Seung-See Lee

Shabnam Ferdowsi

Shaheen Ferdowi

Shan Shan Heh

Shana Chasman

Shannon Galati

Sharif Hraki

Shawn Burs

Shirley Gon-Gibbs

Shubba Kumar

Sidoine Lescauville-
    Tournissac

Simeon Bond

Simonida Benghiat

Sitara Aga

Skye Anne-Smith

Skyler Raskin

Snowden Mark

Sofia Balbuena

Sofia Dossetti

Sofia Lodovico-Hendricks

Sofia Mandich

Sofia Shah

Sofia Wilmore

Sophia Black

Sophia Boris

Sophia Haddad

Sophia Landers

Sophia Parsa

Sophia Pawera

Sophia Rouze

Sophia Soll

Sophie Courion

Sophie Katz

Sophie Kennedy

Sophie Kierszenbaum

Sophie Lascu

Sophie Mark

Sophie Schnebelen

Stacy-Love Belizaire

Stella Gage

Stephan Callas

Stephan Shapiro

Stephane Farenga

Stéphane Karayannis-
    Desbois

Stephane Miaule

Stephanie Crochet

Stephanie Fuller

Stephanie Harper-Smith

Stephanie Lichtenstein

Stephanie Marinello-Silva

Stephanie Mogil

Stephanie Van Quathem

Steven Turnbull

Sunita Bali

Svetlana Bensimon

Svetlana Kouznetsov

Sydney Defranco

Sylvain Sabbah

Taimaru Provensal

Takechiyo Ikuno

Talal Barakat

Talia Lux

Talia Raminfard

Tamara Wagner

Tamaru Provensal

Tanguy Vaz

Tania Feretti-Katz

Tannaz Hamidi-Hashemi

Tanya Abergel

Tara Mavadat

Tara Nahai

Tara-Rei Kitahara
Tatiana Bobin
Tatiana Brenner
Tatiana Safady
Taya Salley
Teia Meigneux
Terence Mongo
Teresa Topaz
Tess Neau
Tessa Boris
Tessa Chad
Tessa Fletcher
Tessa Tingloff
Tevin Franklin
Thadeus Doward
Theodore Boris
Theodore Schellhorn
Théophile Hardy
Thomas Bastien
Thomas Guillaud
Thomas Schnebelen
Thorborn Kaerskov
Tiare Baginski
Tifaine Tojdjmann
Timna Zaray-Mizrahi
Timotee Allouch-
  Chantepie
Timothée Cohen-Roger
Timothy Froehlig
Timothy Hockley
Titiana Shanks
Togo Nagai
Tom Boeken
Tom Caen
Tom Parisot
Tomothée Grimblat
Tong-En Hsiao

Torgen Martinson
Tori Hickey
Trevin Lund
Tristan Harris
Troy Hattler
Tsehay Driscoll
Vaitea Foley
Valdi-Agaelle Belizaire
Valencia Esposti
Valentina Alberti
Valentina Pagliari
Valentina Popeil
Valentine Dessertenne
Valerie Aguirre
Valerie Frechette-
  Cocoluzzi
Valerie Kim
Valérie Vigier
Vanessa Du Basso
Vanessa Marquet
Vanessa Wormser
Vassiliki Economides
Veronica Sabadash
Veronika Vorel
Victor Bertranou
Victor Derycz
Victor Mahe
Victor Parker
Victor Rubin
Victor Shlionsky
Victor Velle
Victoria Brizzi
Victoria Polakoff
Victoria Power
Victoria Simeran
Vincent Rigaud
Virgil Dempsey

Wendy Schnebelen
William Coquillard
William Crowe
William Normand
William Roskin
William Tucker
Wyatt Smith
Xochitl Derycz
Yalda Zakeri
Yann Wollman
Yannick Behrman-Laroche
Yannick Derrien
Yasmeen Al-Faisal
Yasmin Amin
Yasmin Soltani
Ying Chow Yook
Yoann Bohbot
Yohann Bensimon
Yoni Azerad
Youssef Aly
Yusef Seidy
Yusuke Murakami
Zachary Del Duca
Zachary Groper
Zaidal Obagi
Zander Fitzgerald
Zazie Peltier
Zelly Atlan
Zlata Zkharova
Zoe Bortolotti
Zoe Brandt
Zoe Mann
Zoe Salkinder
Zoe Schoenlaub
Zohra Aouragh

I know we've come a long way,
We're changing day to day,
But tell me, where do the children play?

—Cat Stevens

1

MY HOMEWORK WAKES THE NEIGHBORHOOD

Cookies first."

"Homework first."

"Need my cookies upfront, Mom. Otherwise I can't concentrate."

"Okay, one cookie now. Then homework. Then one more cookie."

"Two cookies now. Then homework. Then three more cookies."

"Too many cookies."

"Too much homework."

This is how it usually goes between Mom and me. But today I'm bargaining extra-hard. Dad got off work early and is still in his construction clothes.

"Treehouse?" he says, holding up the plans we drew last summer.

"Homework," I say.

Now while I'm sitting down to twenty-five math problems, an endangered species report, and a language arts packet—action verbs versus linking, can you feel the joy? —*he's* taping our plans back on the fridge. I get to look at them every time I reach for a glass of milk to go with my cookies.

After dinner I help clean up, take a shower, and brush my teeth. I study the week's spelling words, alphabetize my sources for the bibliography, finish writing chapter notes for World History, read twenty pages of *Black Ships Before Troy*, and go over the mistakes on my math quiz. That, I'm happy to say, takes only fifteen minutes. Thanks to my friend Catalina, I got most of them right.

Finally, I sit down at the piano, the one place besides our backyard I want to be. I'm working on a Herbie Hancock song called "Cantaloupe Island." A weird thing happens to me when I play the piano. I'm not in our living room anymore but in my Sound Forest far away. The ground is soft and spongy and full of Dr. Seuss trees, their leaves changing color to the music. Wild birds keep beat on the branches. For Herbie Hancock, the trees turn Popsicle orange, the birds sky blue.

"Sam." Mom's voice breaks in like it's being squeezed through a long tube. "Didn't you have a worksheet on decimals?"

"Already did that," I say, fingers flying across the keys.

2

She holds up the worksheet in front of my song sheet. She flips it over.

There was another side.

My head falls forward and thuds against G, F, C, and a bunch of sharps.

In the middle of the night, I wake up with an anxiety attack. It feels like someone's pounding a drum kit inside my chest. I reach for my phone and tap the meditation app that Bernice recommended.

Bernice is my mom's parenting teacher. Every other month, a group of moms and a few dads go to her house to learn how to be better parents. I don't know what they talk about, but the next day these annoying quotes pop out at us from Mom's mouth. Things like, *You can't prepare the path for the child; you have to prepare the child for the path.* Or, *Empty stomach, empty head.* Or, *Follow through and you won't have to follow up.*

Advice pills, we call them, when Mom's out of range.

"You may be feeling stress from a real deadline," the Guided Meditation Lady says to me in her soft, breathy voice, "or it may be brought on by a self-made pressure."

"It's a real deadline."

"Be mindful of where in your body you're feeling tense."

"Well, I've got sweaty palms, for one. And my stomach feels like I swallowed a shoe."

"Whatever you feel is a natural response to the stress of life. Just let yourself feel those feelings, and they'll melt away."

Easy for her to say. She hasn't seen my homework planner.

I'm not allowed in my parents' room after ten unless it's an emergency, a.k.a. *unexpected situation that demands immediate action*. The dictionary just gave me permission to barge in.

Mom is on her back sound asleep, with her head tilted toward the door. Moms always sleep on the side closest to the door. They're like firemen next to the pole. When a kid cries out in the middle of the night, who comes running?

Not dads. They'll sleep through anything. Even an emergency.

I hover over Mom like a zombie, watching her breathe. She doesn't even have to crack a lid to know I'm there.

"Sam," she whispers, "what's the matter?"

"Bibliography."

"What about it?"

"Forgot."

"You can do it for Wednesday."

"He'll take off points."

She sighs. "A consequence builds character."

Here's something about parents they don't teach in parenting class. When Mom says no, go around to the snoring side of the bed.

"Dad," I whisper. "Wake up."

He sounds like Darth Vader with asthma. I'm surprised he doesn't wake himself up with all that wheezing.

"Dad, need a little help here."

When a mom wakes up in the middle of the night, she does it with the ease of a light switch turning on. A dad wakes up like a guy being electrocuted.

I poke him in the arm.

"*What?! What?! What's the matter?*"

"Bibliography," I say.

In the office, I flip through my stack of index cards, alphabetized by author's last name or, if there's no author, by title. My dad believes kids should take responsibility, but for things that make sense for kids to do, like feeding their pets, fixing their own bikes, or safely operating power tools. Not bibliographies past midnight. So he types for me.

"Hey, Sam," he whispers between sources. "Next Monday is Columbus Day. Three-day weekend. Maybe we can start the treehouse then."

"Maybe," I say. But the truth is, I'm not so sure it's a good idea. Even if we find time to build the thing, when will I play in it?

The office door opens. Mom is standing there with her arms locked across her chest. She looks like an exclamation point.

"He has to have a bibliography," Dad says.

"Sam knew about this project two weeks ago. He should have finished it."

"I did finish. Forgot one thing."

"It's okay to let him fail, you know. Failure is the greenhouse of success."

Then they get into a debate over parenting styles. A LOUD debate, which only ends when the door flies open, and a teenager with purple hair and dark circles under her eyes stares us down.

My big sister, Sadie. Technically, *half* sister Sadie. She's Dad's daughter from his first marriage. Her mom, Emily, died when she was five, which was a tragedy. But some tragedies lead to good things. In this case it led to me. After Sadie's mom died, Dad decided to sell their house.

He fell in love with the realtor.

Guess who the realtor was.

"It's the middle of the night," Sadie says. "Some of us are trying to study."

Note that she did not say *some of us are trying to sleep,* which would be a healthy response from a teenager at two in the morning. If you think I have it bad, you should see how much homework Sadie gets. On average, four hours a night. She's in the HGM Program at North Hollywood High. It stands for "Highly Gifted Magnet," and you have to score in the 99.5th percentile on standardized tests to get in. On top of that, she's captain of the speech and debate team, does mock trial twice a year, and has a bunch of essays to write because she's a twelfth-grader applying to college.

No wonder she drinks coffee at night.

Sadie stomps back to her room and slams the door. The slam sets off a massive explosion in the kitchen. It sounds like a cross between a car alarm and a night full of hungry coyotes.

You wouldn't think two small dogs could make this much noise. But Lucy and Mollie, our twin terriers, yip and howl whenever they hear a high C on the piano or a stranger at the door.

Or their pack wide-awake in the middle of the night.

While *our* dogs are causing all the *other* dogs in the zip code to howl, the phone rings. My bibliography just woke the neighborhood.

"Hello?" Dad says. "Yes, Mr. Kalman, I know what time it is."

It's the old man across the street. He's a retired lawyer, and believe me, you don't want to annoy him.

"No, I don't know how many sleeping pills you took four hours ago. Three, huh? Twenty-seven left in the bottle. Yes, I agree twenty-seven would be a fatal dose for two small dogs."

If Mr. Kalman gets anywhere near their bowls, Lucy and Mollie will be stiffs.

2

I STAND ON A DESK

Next morning before school we line up for handball. There's Jaesang, Catalina, Alistair, and me. The Fab Four of Reed Middle School. Jaesang's a sports genius — he knows every stat of every player of just about every league. On Career Day he announced his plans to own the Lakers someday. I like that about Jaesang. He dreams big. He promised me my own skybox at Staples Center. *That's* a friend.

Every day we thank our stars for Catalina. She's like our very own math tutor, only better because she helps us for free and explains math in a way kids understand. She loves numbers so much, when she heard there would be a pi contest next March, she set her goal of learning a thousand digits past the decimal. She wants to beat the eighth-grade boys.

Cat doesn't do math just in her head. She even does it in

her hair. At least two feet long, dark and wavy and wild if she'd leave it alone. But her *abuelita* tames her hair, braiding it into one long rope.

"It's the power of three, Sam," she tells me. "*Una cuerda de tres hebras no se rompe rápido.* A three-strand rope is not easily broken."

Alistair is our resident goofball and the most disorganized person on the planet. If not for his hands, arms, knees, and toes—on hot days he wears sandals—he'd never remember a thing. Early on his mom taught him to write stuff down. But Post-its and planners don't work for Alistair. There's only one surface he can count on not losing, and that's his own skin.

But put him in a kitchen, and my friend Alistair remembers everything, down to how many teaspoons of vanilla are in his red velvet cupcakes. Weird how people keep track of the things they love.

"You watch *MasterChef Junior* last night?" Alistair says. "They've got this Louisiana girl on. Man, can she flambé! Brought the judges to their knees. Literally."

"How do you have time for *MasterChef Junior* with all the homework we get?"

"I watch while I do my homework."

"Your mom lets you?" Jaesang asks.

"I showed her this article from the *LA Times.* It's all about how the multitasking brain learns better."

"When do you have time to read the paper?"

"Once a day. When I'm pooping."

"*Alistair!*" we all groan.

"What's wrong with pooping?" he says. "It's the final step of a great meal."

I'm in next against Jaesang, but I might as well go straight to the back of the line. For a kid who looks like he's made of toothpicks, Jaesang will surprise you. He's like a praying mantis. They can carry ten times their own weight. Someday Jaesang will too.

His slicey puts me out, and I head for the back of the line. But then I notice that the door to the auditorium isn't closed all the way, and I've still got Herbie Hancock in my head, so I walk over.

Our school piano's old and a little out of tune. But it's a piano. Soon my fingers are flying and I'm back in my grove of Dr. Seuss trees with purple, yellow, and bright orange leaves. Something about this song makes the whole world pop.

When I finish, I hear applause. I look around and there's Mr. Trotter, our music teacher, in his wool cap and white beard. He speaks in a brogue — what he calls his Irish accent.

"Well, Sam, I'd say I've made the right choice."

"Choice for what?"

"There's room for just one solo in the winter program. I picked you."

A sixth-grader has never gotten the solo before. I feel like jumping so high, I'll land on Jaesang's future team.

. . .

In class we do a worksheet on the Code of Hammurabi. It's this ancient tablet from four thousand years ago with 282 of the harshest laws in history. It's where we get the saying "an eye for an eye and a tooth for a tooth." According to the Code, if you were a surgeon and your knife slipped and you accidentally killed a patient, you'd have both your hands cut off. If you were adopted and said to your mom, *You're not my mother*, you'd have your tongue cut out. And if you were a builder, like my dad, and a house you built collapsed and killed the owner's son, *your* son would be put to death.

Just when I'm thinking how glad I am that nowadays we have building inspectors, Mr. Powell makes an announcement.

"I know you're all excited for the Columbus Day weekend," he says. And it's true. Columbus is our favorite explorer because he comes with a Monday off.

"But," our teacher goes on, and Alistair and I swap a smile.

"There's always a butt," I say.

"Some bigger than others," Alistair says. He does his in-chair version of the Truffle Shuffle from *The Goonies*.

And here it comes. "You'll be taking a practice CAASPP test next week, so I'm sending home a review packet."

The CAASPP test. You probably know it as the California Assessment of Student Performance and Progress. We call it the GASP test because it makes it hard for us to breathe.

Mr. Powell goes around the room, dropping these mega-packets on everyone's desk. They sound like someone getting spanked.

Thwack. Thwack. Thwack.

Catalina puts up her hand. "We already have a Lit Circle project for Miss Lopez."

"My review packets shouldn't take you more than an hour a day."

Thwack.

"What about our endangered species report for Mr. Dane?" Alistair calls out.

"Those were on the calendar for today. Didn't you bring yours?"

Thwack.

The problem with Alistair's note-taking system is that at some point during the week, he takes a shower.

Jaesang tells Mr. Powell that he's flying to Seattle to visit his grandparents for the long weekend.

"Good. They can quiz you on prepositional phrases."

"They're from Korea. They don't speak English."

"Maybe you'll sit next to a native English speaker on the plane."

Thwack.

He makes his way around the classroom, dropping the

packets on desk after desk after desk, kids flinching at every *thwack*.

I think about my dad sitting in *his* sixth-grade classroom when he was a boy. Back then kids hardly ever had homework. Soon as the bell rang, they were free.

Free to have fun.

Free to play with friends.

Free to build treehouses with their dads.

A tiny word starts to form in my mouth. Two letters. One syllable. Don't ask me how. It just comes.

"No," I say.

"No?" Mr. Powell repeats.

"No more. It's been like this since third grade."

Some force grabs hold of my hand. It tears a sheet of paper from my spiral. And I watch my hand write two block letters: *HW.*

Then I draw a big circle around them. And a slash through the center.

I hold up my sign.

There are thirty-six kids in the room; only half can see. I climb up onto the desk. Now they all can.

I don't know what the Code of Hammurabi would say about a kid who refuses to write down his homework. Probably I'd have *something* chopped off, but right now I don't care.

Mr. Powell stares at me but speaks to the room. "Class, take out your planners. Write the homework down."

Everyone looks at me for what to do. Like now I'm in charge? I just hold up my sign.

Catalina rips a sheet of paper from her spiral, writes something, and holds it up.

The same symbol, only in neater handwriting.

Jaesang flips the worksheet over, writes the no homework symbol, and leaps to his feet with the sign held high.

Alistair jots one across his palm with his Sharpie, jumps up, and thrusts it out, his hand sweeping across the room so everyone sees.

Other kids join in. Worksheets, notebook paper, the backs of quizzes. All get turned into NO HOMEWORK signs held high.

All of a sudden I feel tall. Not just standing-on-a-desk tall, but superhero tall. Tall on the inside and in the eyes of my class.

They're looking up to me. No one ever has before.

That's when I see the scary face in the window of the door. The face belongs to Mr. Hill, our school principal. If you ran into him at Trader Joe's the way I did once, in line for a free sample, he'd seem all friendly in his Saturday shorts and knee-high socks. But here, in a suit and tie, he's the madman at your window. The monster under your bed.

The door swings open. The monster is in the room.

"Mr. Powell," he says with perfect Principal Calm. "Why is Sam standing on the desk?"

"Sam has had enough of homework, Mr. Hill. He doesn't want to write the assignment down."

"Doesn't he?"

Mr. Hill walks over. It's not every day a sixth-grader is taller than the principal. He stands about eye level to Schroeder and Snoopy on my favorite T-shirt.

"Any student who refuses to write down the homework will be suspended from school. Three days. And the suspension goes on your permanent record."

The words "permanent record" hang in the room.

Alistair sighs. "Sorry, Sam, but if I get suspended, I'll lose kitchen privileges."

Which for Alistair would be like any other boy losing video games. He sits and scribbles the homework on his arm.

Jaesang looks at me. I see his face go all soft, like a ball losing its air. "My mom won't let me go to Seattle."

He sinks to his seat and opens his planner.

One by one, the signs go down. One by one, the students go down too.

Pretty soon it's just me and Catalina on our feet. The other day she told us how homework got her in trouble with God. Every Sunday her family goes to Iglesia del Dios Vivo, Columna y Apoyo de la Verdad, La Luz del Mundo — La Luz del Mundo for short. The congregation is huge. More than a thousand people were listening to the *ministero* and reading along in their prayer books.

Then came the time for silent prayer. The same thousand people in total God-inspired silence.

Except for Catalina's *abuelita*, who was sitting beside her and happened to peek at what no one else could see.

The book her granddaughter was reading in church.

It wasn't the prayer book.

It wasn't the Bible.

It wasn't a book of hymns.

It was *World History: Ancient Civilizations.* Written by so many people, their names don't fit on the spine.

"Ai, Catalina! Qué está leyendo en iglesia?"

Nine hundred ninety-eight heads spun toward them. Plus the minister and all the heads in the choir.

"Un libro, Abuelita. Por escuela." Then she turned to the minister and said, *"Perdóname, Papá. Un montón de tarea para mañana."*

Which, in case you don't know Spanish, means "a mountain of homework due tomorrow."

So I'm thinking, if homework got Catalina in trouble with God, maybe God will give her the courage to stand up to homework.

She sighs. A *montón* of air comes out. Like she's been holding her breath since Sunday.

Then she hangs her head, sits, and writes down the homework.

I guess now's the time to cut my losses. I should sit down, copy the homework, play by the rules. There'll probably be an apology to write. Loss of recess. Lunchtime on the bench. I can handle all that.

But can I handle six and a half more years of this? Sixth grade, the rest of middle school, then high school, where the homework's even deadlier? Are we supposed to just go along like that guy in the Greek myth, pushing the rock up the mountain only to have it roll back down again?

I don't think so. I stay on my feet.

Principal Hill pulls out his secret weapon. "A student who's been suspended may not perform in the winter program."

He just axed down all my trees.

Not me, though. I'm still standing.

3

THINKING IT THROUGH

When Dad loses his temper, Mom reminds him to *take it in before you let it out.* She means he should take in the big picture, see what he's angry about and if it really matters, and then, if it does, go ahead and have a tantrum. Or when Sadie complains that she's got too much stress from debate team, mock trial, homework, and college applications, Mom tells her to *keep your eye on the end zone*, which is perfect for Sadie because the one thing she does for fun is watch football on the couch with Dad. And whenever I'm about to do something impulsive like reach for a seventh cookie, Mom quietly reminds me to *think it through, Sam.*

Think it through. All the way to tomorrow morning, when you wake up with a stomachache.

Think it through. All the way to your next piano lesson and how you'll feel if you didn't learn the song.

Think it through. All the way to this afternoon, when the email makes it home before you do.

"A three-day suspension?!" Mom says.

I guess I didn't think things through.

"There goes your chance of getting into a decent high school," Sadie butts in. That's a sister for you. Helpful, isn't she?

Mom sighs her dragon sigh. "You will write an apology to Mr. Hill, Mr. Powell, and the class. And you will make up all the work you're going to miss."

But Dad defends me. "Why are they giving so much homework anyway?" he says. "We didn't have homework when we were in sixth grade. And we turned out just fine."

Sadie tilts her head as if to say she's not so sure about that.

"It's a different world now," Mom says. "More challenging. More competitive."

"When's the last time Sam played outside with his friends?" I hear Dad say. "When's the last time he built anything with me?"

"All the other kids are doing homework. Do you want Sam to fall behind?"

"All the other parents have lost their minds. Should we lose ours too?"

They ping-pong it back and forth like this for a while. Then Dad makes an astonishing, *you-go-Dad* declaration that warms my heart.

"From now on there will be no more homework in this house!" he says. "I forbid it!"

Would you trade this dad to another family? I wouldn't.

"Really?" Mom says. "Okay, so if Sam doesn't do his homework, he won't get all As on his report card. If he doesn't get all As on his report card — Sadie's right — he won't get into a good high school. If he doesn't get into a good high school, he'll land at a third-rate college, where he'll graduate deep in debt with a worthless degree. If he graduates deep in debt with a worthless degree, he won't be able to find a decent job, attract a wife, or support any kids. So, if he doesn't do his homework, your only son will grow old miserable and alone, and that'll be the end of your family line."

Wow, she really thought that through!

"What about Sadie?" Dad asks.

"I'm not sure I want to have kids. They create too big of a carbon footprint."

Dad turns to me, gives me a straight-on father-to-son look, and says, "Sam, go do your homework."

If I owned this team, he'd be a free agent now.

After dinner I Skype with Alistair.

"Will I be needing a suit for your funeral?" he asks.

"Mine is a fate worse than death," I tell him. "It's homework."

I ask him for the assignments. He says he's not sure I want to hear.

"After you got thrown out, Mr. Powell teamed up with all our other teachers. They went on a rampage."

"Just give it to me straight," I say. "The whole list."

Onscreen, I see Alistair push up his sleeve. He reads the first assignment from his arm. "Science, chapter three, on volcanoes. Do chapter review and connections."

He pushes up his sleeve a little more. "Read up to page forty-seven in *Black Ships Before Troy*—that book gives me nightmares—and do a character chart."

"Anything else?" I ask.

"There's one on my left leg."

He hikes up his pant leg. "Flash cards. We have to look up definitions and draw vocabulary pictures."

"How many words?"

"Twenty-five."

"Anything else?"

Alistair's pant leg comes up over his knee. I can see the scar from when he rolled down his backyard slope and struck a sprinkler head.

"Remember the early humans diorama that's due before Christmas?"

"Yeah."

"Now it's due before Thanksgiving."

"Terrific. Anything else?"

"Hang on. Got to check one more place."

He steps away from the computer, untucks his shirt, and yanks it up. Alistair's been known to write reminders across his stomach, too.

Lucky for me, it's just his face that pops back onscreen. "Nope," he says, "that was just an itch."

"Thanks, Alistair. Glad I Skyped you before you took a shower."

And we hang up.

Day one of my suspension is actually kind of nice. I get to sleep in on a Wednesday. Around nine thirty I roll out of bed, head to the kitchen, and pour myself a bowl of Lucky Charms. Lucky Charms are supposed to be a rare breakfast treat, but with all the work I'll be doing, I'm giving myself permission to eat the whole box.

There's a Post-it from Mom on the fridge: "Gone to a caravan. Home by noon. Get some work done!"

A caravan is an open house just for real estate agents. So they can see what's new on the market and spread the word. Once, when I was home sick on a Wednesday, I got to go with her. I noticed how all the agents seemed more interested in test scores than in house things like countertops, termites, or if the yard had room for a pool.

"Reed has some of the highest scores in the city," Mom always says. "Among the top ten in the state."

Seems to me, if our test scores are driving up the home

prices in the neighborhood, we should get a cut of the money every time a house sells. I tried to tell Mom that, but she said those ideas are better kept to myself.

Then she gave me a cookie.

At ten I look out the window and see Mr. Kalman's newspaper in the gutter in front of his house. Mr. Kalman is the oldest living person on our street. His property has the oldest living trees. Mom says he stopped having them trimmed when his wife died. If you were new to the neighborhood, like a temporary mail carrier, you might wonder why there's a mailbox in front of an overgrown lot. Dad says tree trimming is expensive and maybe Mr. Kalman is short on cash. Mom says she doubts that because Mr. Kalman is a retired lawyer.

Since I'm off for the day—and my bibliography woke him the other night—the least I can do for Mr. Kalman is rescue his paper from the gutter sludge. I head across, pick up his paper, and push open the gate on his wooden fence.

His wife used to paint this fence every year on the first day of spring. She'd start at six in the morning and finish at six at night, her floppy yellow hat making its way across the yard like a sun. One time she saw me watching from my window. Her yellow hat tilted back and showed me this big smile on her face. Then she held her paintbrush out to me. I pointed to myself and gave her a look like, *Me? You want me to help paint?* Her yellow hat waved up and down.

You've never seen a boy who just turned five tie his

shoes so fast. When I got outside, she was waiting for me on our driveway.

"But I'm just a kid, Mrs. Kalman. I don't know how to paint a fence."

"A kid can learn to do anything, Sam," she said.

Her hand held my hand, and my hand held the brush, and together we turned the fence white again.

I carry Mr. Kalman's *LA Times* up to his front door. The path used to have sunlight and shadows. Now it's all shadows.

I knock on the door hard because he might not have his hearing aid in. It takes him about as long as it takes me to brush my teeth before the door opens. Mr. Kalman stands there in a long T-shirt, sagging track pants, and old slippers. I'm pretty sure he wore something spiffier when he went to court.

He puts up a finger because he's on the phone.

"You keep a man on hold? What if there's a gun to his head? No, there's no gun to my head. That was a hypothetical question. Fact of the matter is, I'm calling to report a theft. My *LA Times*."

"Mr. Kalman," I say, but he turns away.

"It wasn't on my driveway this morning."

I tap him on the shoulder. He doesn't turn around.

"Well, could you at least send a patrol car around tomorrow morning at, say, five thirty? Patrol car is a deterrent to this sort of crime."

"Mr. Kalman!" I say again, jumping up and down and waving the plastic-wrapped newspaper at him.

He gives the dispatcher his address. "Otsego with two Os, beginning and end. It's a Native American word meaning 'rock,' or 'place of rendezvous.' Thank you for providing good value for my tax dollars."

Then he hangs up and turns around.

And sees what I'm holding in my hands.

"*You're* the thief who stole my *LA Times*?"

"I didn't steal it. I got it out of the gutter. Thought I'd save you from bending over."

"You're worse than a thief, then. A murderer."

"How so?"

"Deprive a man of his daily exercise and you shave years off his life."

"I was only trying to —"

"I don't need any help."

"Fine!" I say. "I'll put it back where I found it."

I haul back and hurl the paper onto the driveway. It skids into the gutter right where the delivery boy left it.

Man, that felt good!

I step off the creaky old porch of this cranky old man. He calls after me.

"What are you doing home anyway? You're a school-age boy who's supposed to be in school."

"I got suspended."

"No kidding. What for?"

"Refusing to do homework."

He puts a hand to his forehead. It's got nothing to do with a headache. Just his way of thinking.

"They give you a hearing?"

"A what?"

"A hearing. Did they inform you of the charges and give you an opportunity to respond?"

"No. They just threw me out."

"Go back to school tomorrow."

"I can't. I told you, I'm suspended. Not allowed back for the rest of the week."

"If they didn't give you a hearing, it's unconstitutional. *Goss v. Lopez.* Look it up."

4

HOW TO ANNOY
A BIG SISTER

I **consider myself** a pretty good reader. I've read all the Diary of a Wimpy Kid books, half of Harry Potter, and *Shiloh*, book 1. I'm partway through *Black Ships Before Troy: The Story of the Iliad*, even though the long words are making me dizzy and the violence is making me sick. I never miss an issue of *Mad* magazine, and I score in the 80th percentile on the reading part of the CAASPP. Not bad for a kid who'd rather be playing piano.

But this *Goss v. Lopez* business is way over my head. I download and print a PDF of the case and try to read it: *The State is constrained to recognize a student's legitimate entitlement to a public education as a property interest which is protected by the Due Process Clause and which may not be taken away for misconduct without adherence to the minimum procedures required by that Clause.*

You could score in the 90th percentile and still not get what it means.

But if you scored in the 99.5th . . .

Sadie spends most of her time in her room. According to Bernice, teenagers naturally withdraw from the family. It's how they practice being independent.

Her dirty dishes spend a lot of time in there, too. If I were an insect or a rodent, I would definitely live in Sadie's room. For furniture it's got plates with bits of cheese stuck to them and crusts of half-eaten sandwiches hanging off the edge. If you get thirsty, there's always the last sip of coffee sludge at the bottom of the mug. And if you feel like taking a nap, there's a mound of stinky laundry you can snuggle into. The perfect habitat for anything with a tail.

I, however, am never allowed in her room.

But I used to be. When I was younger, she would leave the door open for me. Sometimes she'd even let me sleep on her floor. In the morning, she'd lift her blanket and we'd snuggle under the covers. We'd make up stories one sentence at a time, and when we had them all worked out, we'd take down the box of Playmobil and turn our stories into stop-motion movies. They always had a boy trapped in a flood, stuck in a tree, or riding his bike too close to a cliff.

After I turned six and Sadie turned twelve, her door closed. A sign went up: NO SIBLINGS ALLOWED. PREMISES UNDER SURVEILLANCE.

With words like that on her door, Sadie's bound to understand *Goss v. Lopez*, right?

I take a deep breath, make my hand into a fist, and tap. You couldn't hear that knock if you had a stethoscope pressed to the other side of the door.

I do a second knock, followed by a harder one, then one more soft one as if to say, *Sorry if that was too loud.*

The door swings open. I stand there pinned by my big sister's eyes.

"Can you translate something for me?"

"What's the source language?"

"English."

"What's the target language?"

"English I can understand."

She puts out a hand. Note, she does not invite me in.

I give her the printout of *Goss v. Lopez*. She looks at it, then at me.

"What is this?"

"Supreme Court decision. Mr. Kalman told me to look it up."

"Why don't you get him to translate it for you?"

"I can't afford him."

"I don't have time for this," she says. "I've got two hundred fifty pages to read for AP English, the SAT to retake on Saturday, a mock trial to prepare for, my Common App essay to write, and a boyfriend I haven't even had time to kiss!"

Which might explain the door that just slammed in my face.

If there's one thing I, Samuel Ellis Warren, am good at, it's turning a "no" into a "yes." Want a later bedtime? Tell your parents you can't fall asleep because you're scared you won't wake up. Even a hint of your untimely death will buy you a half-hour of cuddling. Outraged by the tiny portion of dessert you got? Offer to eat more broccoli, then slip it to your dog when your parent turns away.

Don't have a dog? Beg for one every day. And—this is hard, but it works—practice picking up *other people's dogs' poo*. Do this in front of your parents. Let them see how serious you are about pet chores.

When it comes to getting past your big sister's door, you have to think outside the house. First, I make a sign that says GOSS V. LOPEZ? The period under the question mark is a frowny face to show how desperate I am. I go outside and, using double-sided tape, attach the sign to Dad's telescoping pole (he uses it to change really high light bulbs). I hoist it to Sadie's window and thud it against the glass.

Sadie pulls down her roller shade.

She finds another sign taped to her bathroom window.

While she's in there, I race back inside and slip one more sign under her door. Like Hogwarts owls, my signs keep coming. The message is clear: I won't leave you alone until you explain *Goss v. Lopez.*

Which she finally does. Through the closed door.

She starts by reading aloud. "The State is constrained to recognize a student's legitimate entitlement to a public education as a property interest which is protected by the Due Process Clause and which may not be taken away for misconduct without adherence to the minimum procedures required by that Clause."

"Translation?"

Her door opens. "It means you have the right to an education just the same as if it were a piece of land you owned. And they can't take it away from you without giving you a fair hearing. A chance to tell your side."

She hands me back the printout of the case. "Mr. Kalman's right. You should march in there tomorrow and talk to the principal."

I'm fine talking to kids my age. I'm even fine standing on a desk and holding up a sign. But when it comes to talking, actually talking, to authority figures—the thought gives me an anxiety attack.

"The principal scares me."

"Someone else can talk for you. Mom always takes your side."

"Not about homework."

"Ask Dad, then."

"Mister Softy?"

And then, in a quiet voice, I say, "*You* could talk to the principal for me."

"I'm not your guardian, Sam."

"But you're my sister. And captain of the debate team. And you know all those big words."

I give her the sweetest look a little brother ever gave.

5

THE PRINCIPAL CALLS
ME A MORON

Next morning at breakfast, Mom knows something's up. It's way past eight, when Sadie and Dad should've left the house.

"What are you all doing still home?" she says.

"Going to the job site late today," Dad says.

"I offered to walk Sam to school," Sadie says.

"Sam's not going to school. He's suspended."

"Illegally," Sadie says. "They forgot to give him a hearing."

"Who put that idea into your head?"

"Sam."

"And who put it into yours?"

"Mr. Kalman.

Mom marches across the street without looking both ways. I catch only part of what she tells the oldest living man in our neighborhood, but it isn't pretty. Something about how she'd appreciate it if he wouldn't interfere with how she's raising her kids.

"The boy's entitled to a hearing," Mr. Kalman says.

And she says, "He needs to take responsibility for what he's done."

And he says, "Well, there he goes taking responsibility. He's on his way to school."

Coming to school when you're supposed to be suspended is a bit like showing up at your own funeral. Basketballs stop dribbling. Arm wrestling hands let go. Girl chat drops to a whisper as heads turn my way.

Catalina waves. Jaesang gives me a thumbs-up. Alistair flips up his palms. They're so full of notes, they look like bathroom stalls. He shrugs as if to ask, *What gives?* I shrug back because I'm not sure if anything's going to.

Sadie tells Miss Lochman, the principal's assistant, that we've come to demand a hearing. If it had been up to me, I would have said *request* a hearing, or *beg for* a hearing, or *see if it wouldn't be too much trouble for Mr. Hill, out of the kindness of his heart, to grant us* a hearing. But like I said, I'm no good at talking to authority figures.

Mr. Hill keeps us waiting until after the second bell rings. I can't tell if he's really got important Principal Stuff to do, or if by making us wait he thinks we'll go away. It gives Mom and Dad a chance to park and come inside, so that when he finally does open his door, we all go in together.

Miss Lochman comes in too. With a notebook and a pen.

Mr. Hill starts out all official. "For the record, Sam's parents are here. My assistant, Miss Lochman, is here. Sam is here."

He peers at Sadie in her black jeans, gray T-shirt, leather jacket, and purple-dyed hair. She looks like a truant officer's worst nightmare. Part punk rocker, part vampire groupie, all bad girl.

You shouldn't judge people by the way they look, though. Sadie hates vampire fiction.

"And you are?" Mr. Hill says.

"His advocate slash sister."

Mr. Hill takes a cool look at Sadie. "And it's your opinion, as your brother's *advocate,* that I don't have the right to suspend him?"

"Not without informing him of the charges and letting him respond."

She drops the printout on his desk. *Thwack!*

"*Goss v. Lopez,* 1975. The US Supreme Court held that a student's right to property — in this case, his education — can't be denied without due process."

I'm not trading her, either.

"Sam," Mr. Hill says, "do you know why you were suspended?"

"I didn't want to do my homework?"

"You stood on your desk and urged your classmates to do the same. You were defiant of authority. Disruptive of class."

"An act of civil disobedience," Sadie says.

"Civil disobedience in a classroom is an oxymoron. There is nothing civil about a disobedient boy."

Okay, did the principal just call me a moron? Now I feel really dumb.

"I was only trying to tell Mr. Powell how I feel," I say.

"And how is that?"

I told you, I'm no good at talking to authority figures. But right then Sadie nudges me hard in the ribs. Is that any way to treat a brother?

It works, though. I start to talk.

"It feels like I've done something wrong," I say.

"I'm glad you're admitting it."

"Not that. I mean—"

"You don't think you've done something wrong?"

"No. Well, kind of. But all of us, we feel—"

"You're the one who defied the teacher."

"I know, but—"

"You're the one who disrupted the class."

"Mr. Hill," Sadie says, "it's a hearing. How can Sam be heard if you won't listen?"

He sighs and rolls back in his rolling chair. He folds his arms.

This time all Sadie has to do is nod.

"It feels like we're being punished," I say, "but we don't know why. Did we do something to upset grownups, and that's why we get so much homework? I mean, we come to school, we work all day, we go home, we work all night. Then we wake up and do it all over again. There's no time to just be a kid."

He's quiet for a second, and I start to feel better because I think I've gotten through to him. Maybe now he'll see things from our side of the desk. Maybe he'll let me back in school. Back in the winter program, too.

"Sam," he says, "you're the only sixth-grader in my office right now. Maybe the problem isn't with the homework. Maybe it's with you." Then he says something about how Reed is a great middle school with high standards and high test scores.

"We give a lot of homework because that's what it takes to be number one. And we expect all of our students to be team players. It's not for everyone. There are alternative schools in the district you could go to. Not as rigorous as ours."

"You want to send me away from my friends?"

"You might be happier someplace else."

Everything suddenly looks blurry through my eyes.

"Mr. Hill," Mom says, "I'm sure Sam is willing to make it up to you. He'll write an apology. Won't you, Sam?"

It's the last thing in the world I want to do, but I nod and say I will.

Mr. Hill stands up. In case you're ever in a meeting with a principal, when he stands up, the meeting's over.

"And now that you've had your hearing," he says, "the suspension stands."

A hand grabs my arm. Sadie drags me outside.

I've never seen my big sister this mad at anyone before, not even me. Her face is red, with anger sweat on her upper lip. She's so mad, she's not talking. So we just walk for a while, side by side, toward home.

"It wasn't very nice of him to call me a moron," I say.

"He didn't call you a moron, Sam. He used the word *oxymoron*."

"Is that a zit cream?"

"It's a phrase that contains a paradox, or apparently contradictory ideas that are nonetheless true. Like *jumbo shrimp* or *working vacation*."

"How can you have *jumbo shrimp?* That's like saying *tall midget*. It doesn't make sense."

"According to him, neither does *student protester*. But that's what you are. And you should be proud of it."

Oxymorons must be a high school thing.

We trudge on together, Sadie with her head down, me kicking a rock as I go. Mom and Dad pull up alongside us in the car.

"You gave it your best shot, kids," Dad says, leaning out the window. "Nothing more to be done."

That's my dad for you, real quick to let things go.

"Mr. Hill is right," I say. "Other kids keep up. Why can't I?"

Sadie stops. She puts her hands on my shoulders and turns me toward her. She looks at me like I'm the only other person in the world.

"They don't keep up, Sam. They give up. You're different. You had the guts to say no. I wish I'd had that kind of courage when I was your age."

"But you get straight As."

"So? In fourth grade I stopped drawing. In fifth I quit karate. The last book I read for fun was *The Hunger Games* the summer before sixth grade. The only things I've kept up are mock trial and speech and debate because Mom says they'll look good on my college applications. Everything else, everything I love, I've let go."

She looks up the road and then back at me.

"They stole my childhood, Sam. I'm not going to let them steal yours."

She marches on ahead of me. Only she doesn't go home. She goes across the street.

To Mr. Kalman's house.

She pounds on his front door. By the time it opens, I've caught up to her. Now there are two kids standing on his porch.

"I want to sue the school board," Sadie says.

"On what grounds?" Mr. Kalman asks.

"On the grounds that homework is unconstitutional."

Mr. Kalman looks at her, wondering if she means this. She means it.

"Where's the violation?"

"Child labor laws. Cruel and unusual punishment. I don't know yet. But I'll find one."

"You'll need a lawyer."

She looks straight at him.

"With a current license," he adds.

We stand there. How's he going to say no to two adorable kids? Okay, one adorable kid and one fierce teenager.

"At my age?" he says. "Are you crazy? I fall asleep in the chair most afternoons. And don't stray very far from the bathroom."

We don't budge.

"They'd laugh us out of court, kids. You under the legal age of relevance and me long past it."

We stand and stare. Sadie's taking the day off from school and I'm basically forced to. So it's not like we'll be going anywhere soon.

But Mr. Kalman looks tired to me. He really is old, and his wife has been gone a long time. Maybe he wants to be left alone.

"I'm sorry," he says. "I wouldn't be able to see it through."

He shuts the door.

Sadie jams her finger into Mr. Kalman's doorbell, which always sticks. The ringer buzzes. And buzzes. And keeps on buzzing until he opens the door and gives the ringer a flick.

"We're not leaving until you say yes."

"There's a law against trespassing. I could have you arrested."

"Your front yard is in violation of the fire code," Sadie shoots back. "We could have you cited."

"Go away. Let an old man live out what's left of his life in peace."

"Oh, please. You're not dying any sooner than we are. Well, maybe a little sooner. But all the more reason you should want to help. It'll give new meaning to your old age."

She's not captain of the debate team for nothing.

Mr. Kalman's eyes narrow and his nostrils flare. "You are an insolent sixteen-year-old who belongs in a house of corrections!"

"Seventeen. And there's no such thing anymore, Mr. Kalman. It's the twenty-first century. Why don't you step outside and live in it?"

Anger sweat glows on *his* upper lip.

"If I were your grandfather, I'd take my cane to your backside."

"If you were my grandfather, you'd be using that cane to march into court to defend the rights of children."

This time, when his door closes, the deadbolt slides shut too.

6

THE MAILBOX WARS

Sadie goes online and searches retirement homes within fifty miles of our zip code. She clicks on "request brochure" and types in Mr. Kalman's name and address.

By Friday he's getting a flood of mail from places like the Golden Villa, Sunset Hall, and Garden of Palms. He's carrying so many brochures from his mailbox to his front door that I'm afraid he'll fall. Then Sadie will be responsible for a broken hip, and I'm pretty sure she doesn't mean to take things that far.

Meanwhile I try the opposite approach. Guilt. Since I'm not allowed back in school until Monday, I go over and tidy up his front walk. I figure when he sees me raking leaves and clipping wild branches in his yard, he'll feel he has to do something for me. Like be my lawyer.

And after three hours of hard physical labor, which I make seem like four by exaggerating my grunts and sighs near his window — "Oh, man, that's a heavy bag of leaves!" Or, "Phew! Sure is hot out here, even in all this shade!" — the door opens, and I think Mr. Kalman's going to offer me a glass of cold water, maybe a snack.

Instead he leaves me a present on his front stoop.

A bag of trash.

And next to that he puts a box of old newspapers with a note on it: "Blue Bin."

Now I'm his gardener *and* his garbage boy. Soon I become his television repairman, too.

"I'm not getting PBS," he says through the window.

"It's channel twenty-eight, but your TV has to be on three," I tell him.

"It is on three. If you don't believe me, come have a look."

I go inside, past the piano that hasn't been played in years, and notice a collection of framed photographs on top of the piano. There's one of Mr. Kalman as a much younger man dressed in a suit and tie, with Mrs. Kalman in a fancy white dress. In other pictures, I see him standing with children and teenagers — not his own, I think, because they don't look at all like him. Unless they're adopted. There are Asian kids, black kids, Hispanic kids, white kids. All of them dressed up, too, like for graduation.

"Your kids, Mr. Kalman?"

"Friends. From long ago. Now, why isn't my TV working?"

I look at his TV. The cable box is set to 3 and the TV is on 28.

"You've got them backwards," I say, beginning to wonder if he'd be the best lawyer after all. "The TV stays on three."

I set things straight for him and flip on the TV just to be sure. It's a weekday morning, and *Arthur* is on.

"I used to love that show," I say. "Reminds me of the good old days when I didn't have *homework!*"

But I'm suspended and probably shouldn't be watching *Arthur,* so I shut it off.

"When you want to turn off the TV," I remind him, "do it at the set. This is just for channels."

I hand him the remote and start to go.

"It won't work," he says.

"It will if you promise to leave the slider switch all the way to the right, on cable."

"I don't mean the TV. I mean all of this. The chores. The unsolicited help. It won't get me to take your case."

He pulls out his wallet.

"You've done a little over three hours of work around here. At the proposed California minimum wage of fifteen bucks an hour, that's forty-five dollars."

He holds out a fifty-dollar bill to me.

"I don't want your money, Mr. Kalman."

"I don't want your charity, Sam. Take it. And stop coming over here."

Mr. Kalman has blue eyes. Blue eyes can be warm and sparkly and remind you of the sea on a clear day. Or they can be a pair of icicles that make you want to look away.

I look away.

But first I pluck the fifty from his hand.

"Now go on home," he says.

"That's exactly where I'm headed. See . . . I'm walking out your squeaky door . . . picking up my dad's tools . . . heading down your crumbly path . . ."

I swing open the gate.

"Through your wobbly gate now . . . stepping over the paint chips . . . past your crooked mailbox . . . across the street . . . and home!"

I slam our front door. Lucy and Mollie start to yip. I hope they keep it up all the way through his nap.

I spend the rest of the day plowing through to the end of Alistair's Homework Hit List. By the time Mom comes in to say good night, my brain is exhausted, my butt is exhausted, my hand is exhausted.

"Did you write the apology to Mr. Hill?"

"I will, Mom," I say. "I promise. But right now I need to sleep."

I tap my cell phone. The Meditation Lady tells me to breathe.

• • •

Saturday morning, something—I don't know what—wakes me early. I look out the window, across the street, to Mr. Kalman's. Since I trimmed his branches back, you can see his fence, and it's looking pretty shabby. I guess nobody's touched it in five years.

I put on my shoes and walk the dogs around the block. All the other front yards are tidy behind clean, well-kept fences. Ours is too, in the same shade of white Mrs. Kalman used to paint hers.

It was a running joke between her and Dad. Every year they'd talk about changing the color. Every year they'd end up sticking with white.

We've still got gallons of that paint in the shed.

Mr. Kalman told me to stay away from his house. But the fence is at the property line and faces the street. Besides, it's not even his fence.

He never took care of it.

She did.

I start at six o'clock and make my way slowly along the outside, the street side, first. By eleven I peek in through his living room window and see him in his recliner with his glasses on. He's watching PBS.

By two o'clock I've made it all the way around the inside, and all that's left is the gate. I give it a nice clean coat. Soon I hear the mail truck squeak to a stop in front of our house.

The engine purrs there for thirty seconds, which means a lot of mail in our box today. Finally I hear the mailbox door clap shut and the truck drive away.

Sadie must've heard it too. She comes out of our house, sees me across the street with a paintbrush in my hand, and just shakes her head like I'm an idiot.

She unloads the mail. Unloads more mail. Unloads *more* mail. I didn't know our box was that big.

Finally she reaches the end. She opens one of the envelopes, and her face goes all frowny.

She opens another. And another. And with each one, I see her face getting tighter, madder, and, well, frownier.

She looks up. Her twin lasers land on Mr. Kalman's house.

Sadie barrels across the street and kicks open the gate. She marches up to the front door and pounds louder than his TV.

Mr. Kalman opens fast, as if he was hoping for her knock.

"Did the mail come?"

She reads out loud from a brochure in her hand. "Blue Ridge Academy is a therapeutic wilderness program for teens aged thirteen to seventeen who are struggling with defiant behavior or other emotional issues."

She reads another. "Island View is a residential treatment center for teenage girls that focuses on oppositional behaviors."

Mr. Kalman just stands there, grinning.

"*You* sent them?!"

"You'd be surprised what one phone call can accomplish in the twenty-first century."

Now I really want this guy to be my lawyer!

"It's not funny, Mr. Kalman."

"Neither is this."

He holds up *his* stack from the retirement homes.

"I guess we're even," Sadie says.

"I guess so," he says, tossing the retirement home brochures onto his bench. That's when he looks past her and sees me standing at the gate with a wet paintbrush in my hand.

"I thought I said no more chores."

He comes out onto his porch and down the steps like he's about to run me off his land, or worse. But before he gets to me, he notices the fence.

White the way it used to be. The way it hasn't been in five years.

The fresh paint stops him cold.

"I didn't do it for you," I say. "I did it for her."

"Her?"

"Mrs. Kalman. She let me help her once, when I was too small to see over the top."

He walks slowly along the whole inside. He leans over the top to see the whole outside. When he turns back to me, he looks pale. Like instead of seeing a fence, he just saw a ghost.

"Why did you do it?" he asks.

"I don't know. Because it needed to be done, I guess. And because you can't do it yourself."

He brings his hand to his forehead. Also to his eyes. The color in his face comes flooding back. From anger or something else, I can't tell.

Then, pointing to the gate, he says, "You missed a spot."

"That's Sadie's fault. It's where she kicked it open."

He glances at her purple Vans. Purple with a white smudge. He comes over to me, takes the paintbrush out of my hand, dips it in the tray, and leans low to touch up the gate.

He takes his time.

When he's done, he says, "I can't promise we'll win."

"What?"

"I can't even promise we'll get on the docket."

"Huh?"

He stands up now and looks straight at us. "If you still want me to, I'd like to file a lawsuit on your behalf, Sam. Against the Board of Education."

"Why, Mr. Kalman?"

"Because it needs to be done. And you can't do it yourself."

"You mean it?" I say. "You'll be my lawyer?"

"Yes, Sam, I'll be your lawyer."

Sadie and I have the same urge to throw our arms around Mr. Kalman. But too big a hug might tip him over, and that would be the end of our lawsuit. So instead we pat him warmly about twenty times on each shoulder.

He turns to Sadie. "We're going to need some help."

7

WE BUILD A TEAM

Mr. Kalman," Sadie says, "this is Sean, my speech and debate partner."

"And, Mr. Kalman," I say, "this is Alistair, Jaesang, and Catalina. My handball team."

Sean is seventeen and has a full beard. Sadie says school never came easy to him because he had a hard time reading. He's in the regular school, not the Highly Gifted Magnet, at North Hollywood High, and even though he has a C average, he's supersmart—on the speech and debate *and* the Academic Decathlon teams. He's also an ace at technology. But most of all he loves my sister.

Sean opens his laptop. "Where's your router, sir?" he asks.

"End of the hall, last door on the right," Mr. Kalman says. "And don't forget to flush."

We stare at Mr. Kalman like he's from another planet. Or century, which of course he is.

Sadie translates. "Sean means your wireless, Mr. Kalman. You do have an Internet connection, don't you?"

Mr. Kalman shrugs. "I've got cable."

We call the phone company to update our neighbor. The first available appointment is a week from now, but Sadie asks to speak with a supervisor. She says she's the primary caregiver for an old man next in line for a heart transplant. They need a fast Internet connection so that his vital signs can be monitored by the hospital at all times.

An hour later, a tech guy shows up with a Google Fiber line. "It's the most bandwidth you can get," he says.

Mr. Kalman, who's thinner than a ten-year-old's wallet, says, "Do I look like I need a lot of bandwidth?"

While the tech guy gets to work, we gather around Mr. Kalman. I don't think he's had this many people in his house since his gin rummy friends were alive. He sits in his TV chair with a yellow legal pad in his lap and asks us to tell him, one by one, why we're fed up with homework. "I want to hear from all of you," he says.

There's a long, unrushed silence as we think about this.

"It's like a punishment," Alistair says. "Cruel and unusual punishment. Isn't that against the law?"

"Grownups get a break at the end of their workday," I say. "Why don't we?"

"Whenever my grandpa comes to LA," Jaesang says, "we like to go to the Lakers games together. Sometimes I have to skip because of homework."

Catalina, who rides the bus to school from her apartment near downtown, says there's no one at home to help. "The math is easy," she says, "but the language arts packets can get hard. My *abuelita*, she only speaks Spanish. And my parents come home too tired to help."

"Some of it's just a waste of time," Alistair says. "My little sister was pounding the table last night. She had to find the word *school* twenty-five times in a word search. She could only find twenty-two. Those backwards diagonals are killers."

"Plus," he adds, "they make us do Delta Math online. If you get one problem wrong, you have to go back to the start and do it all over again. Last night I got all the way to thirteen out of fifteen, made one carrying error, and got sent back to number one."

The high school kids are getting slammed even worse. "I haven't been to soccer practice in a month," Sean says.

"I'm putting in four hours a night," Sadie says.

Sean tells us he sleeps only on the weekends. "Something's got to give," he says. "For me it's sleep."

Sadie looks at him for a second like they're the only ones in the room. "For me it's you," she says.

Now it's Mr. Kalman's turn to talk. He tells us that a lawsuit is like a war. We're David and the school board is

Goliath. "Only," he says, "we can't even afford the slingshot. So we're going to have to raise some money."

"You're going to charge your own neighbor?" I say, thinking maybe I ought to trade *him*.

"The money's not for me, Sam," he says. "It's for the case. What we're filing here is a class action lawsuit. That means *you're* going to court to represent all the kids who have the same complaint."

"I am?"

Sadie explains. "It's like in Prisoner, Sam. When your whole team is out and you're the only one still in, you can yell 'Jailbreak!' And if you win that point, the rest of the team is set free. The same is true in a class action lawsuit. You're one person, but you can set everyone else free."

That's a whole lot of responsibility on the back of one sixth-grade boy.

"But we're kids, Mr. Kalman," Jaesang says. "Who says we even have rights?"

"The Supreme Court, that's who."

He tells us about this fifteen-year-old kid named Jerry Gault who was home one day with a friend, and they thought it would be funny to prank call the lady next door. "This was in Arizona in the mid-1960s," Mr. Kalman explains. "There were some pretty tough laws against obscene telephone calls. The lady was offended by what the boy said, so she called the police, who got the phone company to trace the call. They came and arrested both boys but didn't notify their parents, just took them to Juvy. The judge set the hearing for the next day, but by the time the parents found out, it was too late to get a lawyer. So the court assigned a truant officer to represent the teens. The judge ruled that Jerry Gault was guilty. He sentenced him to six years in a home for delinquent kids."

"Six years!" Alistair says. "That's harsh."

"Not Hammurabi harsh," I say, thinking of Jerry Gault's tongue.

We ask Mr. Kalman what the kid said on the phone.

"It was never proved that he'd said anything. I told you, his friend was on the line too. Mrs. Cook *thought* it was Jerry Gault who'd done the talking, but she offered no evidence. The family tried to appeal, but in those days, a minor had no right to an appeal. So the parents asked the Supreme Court to hear the case. By the time they did, their son was eighteen years old and halfway through his sentence."

"And?"

"The Supreme Court ruled: Jerry Gault had been denied due process — written notice of his hearing, the right to an unbiased attorney, and the right to confront any witnesses against him. 'Under our Constitution,' Justice Fortas wrote, 'the condition of being a boy does not justify a kangaroo court.' The moment those words were written, children were guaranteed constitutional rights under the law."

"Wow," I say.

"Awesome," Catalina says.

"So we do have rights," Jaesang says.

"Yes. But suing for them can cost a pretty penny. And the first thing a judge is going to want to know is whether we have enough resources to take care of the class of plaintiffs. To see the case all the way through, no matter how hard or expensive it gets."

"We could have a bake sale," Alistair suggests.

"You'd have to sell a whole lot of brownies."

Then Sean snaps his fingers with an idea.

"Website."

Sadie looks at him and nods. "We'll build a site that takes online donations. We'll crowdsource the funding."

"That'll never work," Alistair says. "You need PayPal or a credit card to pay for stuff online. Once, I tried to order a pasta maker. Got all the way through the shipping page, and then they asked for my credit card. I had to abandon the cart."

"Kids can pay their parents back with lunch money," Jaesang says. "Who wouldn't eat one less bag of chips to stop homework?"

"Kettle chips or ordinary Lay's?"

We look at Alistair like, *Really?* He shrugs.

"We'll need a catchy name," Sean says, and we toss around ideas.

"Stop homework dot com?"

"Homework sucks dot com?"

But it's Catalina who comes up with the perfect name.

She swings her braid around and grabs it with her left hand. It's her microphone now as she says, "Save our childhood dot com. That's what we're fighting for."

"Dot org," Sean says. "It'll be better for the movement."

We break into teams of two and brainstorm more ways to raise money. I end up with Alistair, who has a hard time focusing.

"Can we sit in the kitchen?" he says. "It'll be quieter there."

Everything about Mr. Kalman's house — including the owner — is original from the 1930s.

His oven clock has hands. The kitchen floors are vinyl and curl up at the corners as if they're trying to get the old man's attention. The wallpaper's curling too — faded yellow sunflowers with tiny pieces of Scotch tape keeping them down.

At the table, I flip the page on my legal pad. The oilcloth is sticky with jam.

"So," I say, "any ideas on how we can raise money?"

Alistair is standing in front of the open fridge. He peels back the plastic wrap on a bowl. "Tuna salad." He leans in for a sniff. "With relish and a hard-boiled egg. Think I can taste some?"

"I think we should be getting to work, Alistair."

"I won't be able to concentrate now that I've sniffed the tuna. Sorry, Sam, but once it's in my nose, it's on my mind. And once on my mind . . ."

He finds a loaf of bread, makes himself a sandwich, and takes a bite.

"Oh, man! When it comes to tuna, the old guy kills it."

This is the problem with partner work. One person wants to work. The other's busy eating a sandwich. And what's he going to want after he's done eating?

I look up, and sure enough, he's got his nose in the milk carton to see if it's fresh.

Gulp, gulp, gulp. Burp. "Ahhhhhhhhh."

Alistair sets down the empty glass. Then he looks at me and says, "Reduce, reuse, recycle."

Reduce, reuse, recycle was our elementary school's Earth Day slogan. Last year everyone had to make conservation posters with those words blazed across the front. The idea was to make the whole community more aware of all the paper and plastic and metal that winds up in the landfill, and all the electricity and food that goes to waste.

On the day after Earth Day, the Dumpster was overflowing with posters.

"What does reduce, reuse, recycle have to do with homework?"

"You'll see. Just stick with me, Sam. And keep me well-fed."

8

WE RAISE A
SMALL FORTUNE

The following week, we get started on Alistair's tuna salad inspiration. When he said "Reduce, reuse, recycle," he meant we'd be reducing the piles of old school projects in people's closets, reusing them for a higher purpose, and recycling them into cash.

We start with every California third-grader's worst nightmare. Outside the gate of Oakdale Elementary, a private school we can walk to, we ask the key question: "Have you done your California Missions Project yet?"

"I wish," one girl says. "That thing's about to ruin my weekend."

The California Missions Project has been known to cause anxiety attacks, hot glue gun injuries, irritable bowel syndrome, and insomnia—and that's just what it does to parents. Kids have suffered from anxiety attacks, hot glue gun injuries, irritable bowel syndrome, insomnia, *and* chronic lower back pain from lugging those things to school.

Here's the rubric that Mrs. Klatchett gave us back in third grade:

You like how size matters more than creativity?

Jaesang got a ninety-eight on his mission. Mrs. Klatchett took off two points because, while he was walking through the classroom door, he tripped and smashed one corner of his model into the wall. It left a quarter-inch dent in the base. "Out of compliance," Mrs. Klatchett said, "with the sixteen-by-sixteen rule."

Still, it's a really nice model of the Santa Barbara Mission. It's even got aqueducts and miniature Chumash Indians. Jaesang had help from his mom. She's a set designer for the movies.

We show his model to the third-grader outside Oakdale.

"How much you want for it?" she asks.

"Fifty bucks," Catalina says. The girl hesitates. She glances around, sees that no teacher is watching, then opens her pink duct tape wallet.

A crowd gathers. I tell them we've got more like it for sale on saveourchildhood.org.

"No credit card required. Cash on delivery."

On Saturday we pound on doors. We ask our neighbors if there are any California Missions Projects lying around, and if so could we collect them for the Museum of Childhood that will be opening next summer in Exposition Park.

Dear Parents:

The California Missions Project is underway! What better way to learn about how the Spanish Missionaries transformed the state than to build a model of one of their 21 missions? Due to limited space in the classroom, models must be TO SCALE on a base foam board of 16" x 16." NO EXCEPTIONS. Any model more than 16 inches square will lose 20 points. Students will need your help to plan the projects and obtain materials, but they do not need your help in constructing the models. Models should be their original work. ABSOLUTELY NO KITS ALLOWED!!!!!

NOTE: ALL WORK ON THIS PROJECT MUST BE DONE AT HOME. DO NOT SEND YOUR STUDENT WITH MATERIALS TO CLASS.

RUBRIC

CHURCH	/20 POINTS
COURTYARD/other buildings	/15 POINTS
SIZE REQUIREMENT	/20 POINTS
MATERIALS	/10 POINTS
ACCURACY	/10 POINTS
LABEL	/10 POINTS
CREATIVITY	/15 POINTS

There's no such thing, of course, but nobody asks. They're thrilled to be emptying out garages, closets, and in some cases, the trunks of cars.

My old Radio Flyer fills up fast. Back at Mr. Kalman's, we sort through all the missions, do a few upgrades on the ones that got Bs and Cs, and then organize them according to name — Santa Barbaras over here, San Joses there, San Rafaels on the couch. By Saturday night we've got thirty-two missions ready to sell.

Then we check our website. Small problem: we have orders for ninety-eight California Missions! Sean says we should just raise the price, but that doesn't seem right to me. And Catalina agrees: "We told kids fifty dollars a mission," she says. "We have to keep our word."

"But we don't have enough supply to meet the demand," Jaesang protests.

Then Sean says the four words that hijack the rest of our weekend.

"We can make more."

Which is crazy because then we'll be doing a ton of homework to stop homework. Wait, is that an oxymoron? Or a paradox? Honestly I can't tell.

Mr. Kalman fires up his 1977 Buick station wagon. Eight cylinders, whitewall tires, and a hideaway seat in the way, way back. "A hundred eighty thousand miles on her and she still purrs," he announces as we pick up speed. You can tell he loves this car.

We're loving it too. Catalina and Alistair are in the way, way back, Sadie and Sean in the middle, and Jaesang and me in the front with Mr. Kalman.

But Jaesang is having a hard time getting the music to play.

"What is this?" he says, holding a small plastic rectangle with two tiny wheels in it and a thin black tape stretched across the front.

"Tea for the Tillerman," Mr. Kalman says. "One of Cat Stevens's best albums."

Jaesang flips it around and holds it up to the window for light.

"Where's the 'on' switch?"

Mr. Kalman smiles. "It doesn't have one. It's a cassette. You slide it into the car stereo and press 'play.'"

We all watch, fascinated, as Jaesang slides the thing called a cassette into a narrow slot in the Buick's dashboard. He recognizes the arrow on one button and presses it, and we hear this long hissing sound through all six of the Buick's speakers.

Then the hissing stops and a guitar starts, a D-major chord, and after that a man's voice breaks in. He sings a song about all the progress humans have made in technology and space travel and skyscrapers, but that also asks, "Where do the children play?" And the more I listen to the words, the more I think we've found our anthem. An anthem for saveourchildhood.org.

Soon we're all singing along. Even Mr. Kalman is singing!

On the way home from Home Depot, with the Buick packed to the max with building supplies and kids, he's still singing.

And back at the house, with Cat Stevens on the stereo now and a fresh batch of Mr. Kalman's tuna salad ("The chopped celery is a great touch," Alistair tells him), we turn Mr. Kalman's dining room into a California Missions factory.

It's an assembly line, with Sean cutting foam core, me breaking balsa wood, and Jaesang painting. Alistair's on the glue gun.

The only missing person is Sadie, who has a mock trial to prepare for.

Catalina calls out orders from our website. "We need three San Juan Capistranos. Five Santa Ineses. Three San Luis Reys."

The funny thing is, nobody's complaining. Maybe because there's a point to what we're doing. Most of the homework we get is just endless math exercises or stupid questions about boring chapters in a textbook. But our work today means something. It feels like we're building more than just models.

Meanwhile, Jaesang and Mr. Kalman are discussing the Lakers.

"You a fan?" Mr. Kalman asks.

"I've loved them since I could lift a basketball, Mr.

Kalman," Jaesang says. "I even stuck with them when they won seventeen and lost sixty-five."

"That's pretty loyal. You collect any cards?"

"I got a few. You?"

"Got a few. Someday we'll have to do a trade."

Jaesang twirls his pad thai noodles, strategizing. "Got any from the seventies?"

"I'd have to look."

Jaesang nods. His long-term goal might be to own the Lakers, but short-term it's to own a set of trading cards from their heyday.

"I'm searching for the 1971–72 starting lineup. Especially the Wilt Chamberlain."

"That's a rare card."

"I know. They won the finals that year."

The following weekend, we switch to science projects. Catalina has a friend who goes to King Middle School. She remembers her saying that King's science fair is going on right now.

I happen to really like science fairs. In theory, you walk around a classroom or a gym, and you learn so much from these projects that were made by kids for kids. But that's not how it really happens. What really happens is the due date shows up like a shark's fin, and as it gets closer and closer, kids get anxiety attacks. Then their parents or tutors or older siblings rush out to Staples for tri-fold boards, glue sticks, and Sharpies, and then they race home to do most of the work. I don't get why we can't just work on them in school. Instead of taking notes on a chapter, or worse, copying from the board, let us actually *do* the research and the science project in school.

On the Monday afternoon after King's science fair, we hang around outside their campus.

Sure enough, at three thirty I see a mobile of the planets floating through the main gate. It's made of painted Styrofoam attached to a curved rod. More projects drift out after it. Big display boards with titles like "How Do Ants Communicate?" "Is Nuclear Power Safe?" "Do Video Games Make You Smarter?"

Catalina and I stand on one corner, Sadie and Sean on another. We offer twenty bucks a project.

Mr. Kalman's Buick fills up fast.

We go online to private schools' websites, click on their calendars, and see when their science fairs are. There's one at Creston Hall in less than a month.

Tuesday morning we target their drop-off line, asking if anyone wants to buy a science fair project. "Only fifty bucks."

We sell out after fifty cars. One mom slips me a hundred-dollar bill and says, "Keep the change. We are so over these projects."

Back at Command Central, Catalina adds up our take.

We all stare at the computer screen like it's a treasure we dug up in our own backyard.

Our grand total: $6,550.00!

My friend Alistair plus Mr. Kalman's tuna salad equals genius!

"Maybe homework's not so bad," Sean says. "We could get rich off this business."

"What about all the poor kids who can't pay?" I say.

"There are enough rich kids who can."

"But that wouldn't be fair," Jaesang points out. "All kids get homework."

"Most can't afford tutors, though," Sadie says.

"Or our educational products," Alistair adds.

"And if both parents are working," Catalina says, "there's no one around to help."

Mr. Kalman, who's been sitting in his chair—sleeping or thinking, I'm not quite sure—suddenly opens his eyes.

"That's it!" he says. "That's an argument we can win. Homework violates the Equal Protection Clause. Kids, I think we have a case."

I'm not sure what the Equal Protection Clause is, but when Mr. Kalman leaps out of his chair, I slide onto his piano bench and start playing jazz.

The piano's out of tune, but my Sound Forest is full of dancing birds.

9

WE GO TO COURT

Technically speaking, ours isn't a case yet. It's a hearing to see if what we've got is worthy of being a case. To get the hearing, first we had to file a claim against the school board.

In my absolute best handwriting, I filled out the claim, saying that I've been harmed by homework. Mr. Kalman sent it in for me.

LOS ANGELES UNIFIED SCHOOL DISTRICT
CLAIM FOR DAMAGES
TO PERSON OR PROPERTY

INSTRUCTIONS:
1. Read entire claim form thoroughly.
2. Fill out claim form completely, as indicated.
3. The claim form must be signed by the claimant (or parent/guardian if claimant is a minor).
4. The filing of a claim form does not guarantee the claim will be paid.

NOTE: PRESENTATION OF A FALSE CLAIM IS A FELONY (PENAL CODE SEC. 72)

CLAIM FORM

RECEIVED
01 NOV

1. Name of Claimant:	
Samuel E. Warren	2. Home Telephone: 818-654-9799
	Business Telephone: I don't have one.

3. Address of Claimant:
1181 Otsego Street Valley Village, CA 91607

4. Name and Address where you wish notices or communications to be sent:
1180 Otsego street, valley Village, CA 91607

5. Claimant's Date of Birth:
March 2

6. Claimant's Social Security No:
You'll have to ask my mom.

7. Date when damage occurred:
It's been going on for years

8. Time when damage occurred:
After school

9. Where did damage or injury occur? (Name of School, Address, Intersection, etc.)
At home. But it's school's fault.

10. Exact/precise location of incident: (N/E corner, location on property, etc.)
My desk, the kitchen table, the bathroom.

11. Describe in detail how damage or injury occurred. (attach additional sheets, diagrams, if necessary)
It started in kindergarten. Teachers gave us work to do at home. They called it homework. They said if we didn't do it, there would be a consequence. That was stressfull.

12. Were law enforcement emergency agencies called? Yes ___ No ✓ I wish.

13. If a physician was visited because of this injury:
Date of Visit: Lots of times, Physician's Name: Harold Coleman
Physician's address: 12480 Riverside Drive

14. Why do you believe the Los Angeles Unified School District is responsible?
Because you let teachers give us homework. It makes me anxious and I have to use a meditation app to fall asleep. And I don't have time for my music or my family or my dogs.

Revised 2005

→

15. Names of all District employees involved in this injury or damage:

Mr. Powell

Mr. Hill

Miss Lopez

16. Witnesses to injury or damage. List all persons, with addresses and phone numbers, known to have information: (Attach additional sheet, if necessary)

Alistair Martin   Jenny Warren
Jae-sang Lee   Steve Warren
Catalina Martinez   Sadie Warren

17. List dollar amount of damages incurred to date (attach copies of receipts or estimates)

How do you put a price on childhood?

18. Total dollar amount of damages to date:

It's not the money It's the lost time.

19. Total estimated dollar amount of future damages:

Could be huge.. If it keeps up we'll be too burnt out to work

20. Signature of Claimant or person filing on his/her behalf, (give relationship to claimant):

(PROCHAIN AMI)

_Avi K_____

Date: October 29

21. Print or type name of person listed above

Avi Kalman

Here's the letter they wrote back:

 LOS ANGELES UNIFIED SCHOOL DISTRICT
MEMORANDUM

Mr. Avi Kalman
1180 Otsego Street
Valley Village, CA 91607

November 1

Dear Mr. Kalman:

We have received your Claim for Damages to Sam Warren, a minor and student at Reed Middle School. Under normal circumstances, we would forward this complaint to Livingston Gulch, Counsel for the Los Angeles Unified School District. However, in this matter it is obvious that the boy's Claim is frivolous and hardly merits the time I have put into writing this response.

Homework is a long-standing feature of a child's education. Like it or not, it's here to stay.

Sincerely,

[signature]

Maynard Phillips
Executive Officer
Los Angeles Unified School District

P.S. In case you missed the note on page 1 of our form: "Presentation of a False Claim is a felony (penal code sec. 72).

333 SOUTH BEAUDRY AVENUE, LOS ANGELES, CA 90017

When the letter came, Mr. Kalman asked me if I was upset by it.

"Wouldn't you be?" I said.

"Nope. It's exactly what I hoped for. If they had taken your complaint seriously, they would have had forty-five days to respond. By rejecting it out of hand, they've given us standing to sue."

That's how we got our hearing so fast. But I know how hearings go, and I'm not looking forward to this one.

When it comes to scary places, the principal's office is like It's a Small World compared with a federal courthouse, which is the Twilight Zone Tower of Terror. At the courthouse, everyone wears a suit and carries a briefcase. Even the criminals dress up, so it's hard to tell who's who.

We're dressed up too. Mr. Kalman insisted. "My team has to look presentable in court," he said. Sadie and Sean look like they're off to their first real jobs. Sean even trimmed his beard for the occasion. And Jaesang, Catalina, Alistair, and I look like we're going to our high school graduation, which is what Mr. Kalman told our parents when he offered to take us shopping.

"I'm just getting them outfitted for their high school graduation," he said.

"Mr. Kalman," Mom pointed out, "they're sixth-graders. They're going to grow between now and high school."

"I certainly hope so," he said.

Then he took us to the Hollywood Suit Outlet for the boys and to Macy's for the girls.

Sadie objected, saying that "gender is a social construct" and *she* wanted to shop at the Hollywood Suit Outlet too. Mr. Kalman said, "You're right. You can shop wherever you want."

But the suits at Macy's fit her better, so she got hers there.

We make our way up a series of escalators to the fifth floor. For Sadie, the federal courthouse isn't so scary. She's already been here multiple times.

"This is where we do mock trial," Sadie says.

"How long have you been doing that?" Mr. Kalman asks.

"Three years. Since ninth grade."

And she's good at it, too. In her last case the real judge who was volunteering for the mock trial said Sadie showed "true grace under pressure" in her cross-examination of the defendant. "I see a lot of professional attorneys in this courtroom," he said. "They could learn a thing or two from you."

That really made Sadie's day.

So not only does she know how to find room 527, where our case is going to be heard, but she's also feeling right at home here in federal court.

Unlike in mock trial, in real court there's a lot of waiting around. It's not like you have an appointment to get your team picture taken for soccer. Those people really stick to the schedule. Here it's more like: Show up on the appointed day at ten o'clock and maybe we'll get to your case by four. If not, come back tomorrow and maybe we'll get to your case by noon. If not, come back after lunch and, well, you get the point.

At two thirty the judge, a nice-looking man who's scary only because of his black robe, says, "In the matter of *Warren v. Board of Education*, are the interested parties here?"

"That's us," Mr. Kalman says.

We all stand up and start saying, "Here, Your Honor. Present, sir. Yes, Your Honor," like it's the first day of school and he's calling roll.

The judge has a plaque on his desk that says OTIS WRIGHT III, which means he's Otis Wright the Third. I didn't learn to read Roman numerals from a homework packet, by the way. I learned it from Age of Empires.

Otis Wright the Third looks for the grownup among us, but all he sees are two teens and four eleven-year-olds because Sean stood up in front of Mr. Kalman and he's at least half a foot taller. "Is the attorney of record, Mr. Avi Kalman, present?"

Mr. Kalman steps around Sean. "Yes, Your Honor."

"Filing as *prochain ami* to the minor?"

"Correct, Your Honor."

This is one thing about the law you've got to love. Kids can't sue because we're underage. You can ask your parents to sue for you—as your legal guardians. But Mom refused to be a party to the lawsuit. She said that while she supports me as a parent, she thinks the lawsuit is taking things too far. She also said it might draw too much attention to our family and hurt her business as top realtor in the neighborhood.

Dad said he wouldn't sign on to the lawsuit, but he wouldn't stand in the way, either.

Mr. Kalman said, "We don't need your parents. I'm filing as your *prochain ami*. It's French for 'next friend.'"

Next friend is the legal term for a grownup who takes your side. Every kid ought to have a *prochain ami*, don't you think?

"According to the brief," Judge Otis Wright the Third says, "you are seeking class action status in a complaint against the Board of Education on the grounds that *homework is unconstitutional?*"

"That's correct, Your Honor."

"Forgive my asking, but is your license to practice law current?"

"I sent the check in on Friday."

Mr. Kalman winks at me. I guess that means his license is current.

"Well, for me to certify the class, I have to make a few findings. First, can you afford to see this matter through?"

Catalina barrels forward. I've been watching a lot of legal shows on TV lately. She's supposed to say, "Your Honor, may I approach?" But she's a little overeager and steps right up.

"Here are our financials, sir," she says, handing him a bank statement from the official Save Our Childhood bank account we opened.

Our total take from project flipping so far: $12,247.50. (We did the bake sale, too; Alistair's brownies sold for two bucks apiece.) A big number if you ask me, but Otis Wright the Third doesn't seem so impressed.

He looks the bank statement over, then glances up at Mr. Kalman. "I'm assuming you're taking the case pro bono."

That's another cool legal term. It means taking the case for free. Literally, "for good" in Latin.

Mr. Kalman nods. I knew he'd never charge his across-the-street neighbor.

"That's fine if you win. But if you lose—and lose again on appeal—you'll have to pay attorney's fees to *him*."

Judge Wright points to a very thin man in a very green suit, the snake in the room. Not literally a snake, but one of those people who can stand so still, you hardly know they're there. We didn't even notice him before the judge pointed him out.

He's Livingston Gulch, the lawyer for the Board of Education.

Sadie tells Judge Otis Wright the Third that if he grants us class action status, we'll raise more money. "From the class itself."

"How so?" the judge asks.

"According to the latest census, there are fifty million

students in K through twelve public schools across the country. We'll ask each of them for a dollar. Even if we get just ten percent, it ought to see us through."

Livingston Gulch smiles but doesn't show any teeth. He just stands there very still. Watching. Waiting.

"Which brings me to the next question," Judge Otis Wright the Third says, "numerosity of the class. How many of those students are in the Los Angeles Unified District?"

To get class action status, you have to show that a lot of other people could make the same complaint. Then it makes sense for just one case to represent them all.

"Seven hundred thousand," Sadie says.

In other words, my team's so big, they can't all fit in one courtroom.

"What do you see as the common damages, Mr. Kalman?"

"Violation of child labor laws and privacy rights. Emotional hardship due to unwarranted stress. And unequal protection under the US Constitution."

"Claims you believe are typical of the class, not just your client?"

"We do, Your Honor."

A green sleeve goes up—Livingston Gulch is raising his hand.

"Mr. Gulch?" the judge says like he's calling on a student.

When Gulch speaks, the words tiptoe out of his mouth one by one.

"I move to strike."

"Strike what?"

"The entire premise. This hearing. I move to strike."

"On what grounds?"

"Relevance, Your Honor. The boy's claim has no business in federal court. In 2002, *Board of Education v. Earls*, the Supreme Court affirmed the power of local school boards to choose which courses to offer, which textbooks to teach" —he snaps his head toward Mr. Kalman— "whose urine to test, and, by implication, how much homework to give. Therefore, I move to strike."

Judge Otis Wright the Third looks at Mr. Kalman.

Who looks like he just stepped in something nasty and is afraid to peek at his shoe. But the look doesn't last long.

"In 1969, *Tinker v. Des Moines Independent School District*," Mr. Kalman says, "the justices held that, and I quote: 'Vigilant protection of constitutional freedoms is nowhere more vital than in the community of American schools.' In other words, if the schools take away students' constitutional rights, the federal government can step in and stop them. They did it in *Goss*. They did it in *Tinker*. They did it in *Brown*. And, if necessary, I believe they'll do it here."

Have I mentioned how glad I am that I live across the street from this man?

Livingston Gulch raises his hand again.

"Yes, Mr. Gulch?"

"One swallow does not make a summer."

"I'm sorry?"

"Aristotle. Just as it takes more than one swallow in the June sky to announce the arrival of summer, so it takes more than one anxious, distractible child to make reasonable people believe that homework is bad for all. For every child like this, I can show you thousands more who cope with the demands of the modern world just fine."

He's ten feet away from me. Why do I feel his hand inside my guts, squeezing?

"Well, Mr. Gulch," Justice Otis Wright the Third says, "you're going to have to. In the matter of *Warren v. Board of Education*, class action status is hereby granted."

His gavel clops the block on his desk. Livingston Gulch turns to us. "I'll see you on the next available date." And he slithers out of the courtroom. Really, his feet never leave the floor.

"Now what?" Sadie asks.

"Now we notify the class."

10

GOING VIRAL

According to Catalina, there's this concept in math called the power of doubling. It means you can spread the word really, really fast. You tell 2 people about something and they each tell 2 more. That's 7 people who know.

(You + 2 + 4) = 7

Those 4 each tell 2 and now 15 people know.

(You + 2 + 4 + 8) = 15

The 8 each tell 2 more and now 31 people know.

(You + 2 + 4 + 8 + 16) = 31

The 31 then turns into 63.

(You + 2 + 4 + 8 + 16 + 32) = 63

The 63 jumps to 127.

(You + 2 + 4 + 8 + 16 + 32 + 64) = 127

And the 127 turns into 255.

(You + 2 + 4 + 8 + 16 + 32 + 64 + 128) = 255

All that spread in just a few minutes of telling.

But how many people do you know with only 2 friends? Most of us have at least 10. Watch what happens when you tell 10 people, who tell 10 more, who tell 10 more, who tell 10 more.

(You + 10) = 11
(You + 10 + 100) = 111
(You + 10 + 100 + 1,000) = 1,111
(You + 10 + 100 + 1,000 + 10,000) = 11,111
(You + 10 + 100 + 1,000 + 10,000 + 100,000) =
111,111
(You + 10 + 100 + 1,000 + 10,000 + 100,000 +
1,000,000) = 1,111,111

One million, one hundred eleven thousand, one hundred and eleven! That's how many YouTube hits we get in the first week of our *Stop Homework* video.

Sean and Sadie filmed it in our backyard, with me on a portable keyboard and Jaesang, Catalina, and Alistair singing, "I throw my backpack in the air sometimes / singing, *No-no, no more homework!* / I wanna take a break and live my life / not just slave away every day and night. / We told you once, now we tell you twice, / come on stand with us, we'll protect your rights!"

Then Sadie cued me, and I said, "Hi, I'm Sam Warren and I'm suing the schools to stop homework. If you're a student in LA Unified and you feel that there's just too much homework, then I've got you covered. That's what a class action lawsuit is. I sue. You get to be in my class."

Then I asked them all for a dollar.

The following week the revolution starts. All across the country, kids go on homework strikes. Teachers send us emails begging us to drop the lawsuit. Livingston Gulch asks Judge Otis Wright the Third to shut down saveour childhood.org. He claims it's interfering with students' rights to an education.

Guess what case he cites. *Goss v. Lopez*.

Mr. Kalman counters that our website is an exercise in freedom of speech. He cites a different Supreme Court decision, *Tinker v. Des Moines Independent School District*, which gave students the right to free speech as long as it didn't disrupt classwork.

"But it *does*," Livingston Gulch argues. "Because of their website, kids are refusing to do their homework."

"Homework," Judge Otis Wright the Third says, "not classwork."

So the website stays up. And the money pours in. By the end of the week we've raised a hundred thousand dollars!

On Sunday Mom runs an open house for one of her listings. I go with her because it's a three-bedroom, two-bathroom house with a nice-size yard. "A family house," Mom says as we walk past her picture on the Coldwell Banker sign that announces: JENNY WARREN, TOP SALES FIVE YEARS IN A ROW.

"Nothing sells a family house like the scent of cookies and the sight of kids," she says.

So I'm in this remodeled kitchen doing homework and trying not to eat all the cookies she baked when who shows up — out of his suit and tie — but Mr. Hill. I didn't know he was looking to buy a house in the neighborhood.

"Hello, Mr. Hill," I say.

"Hello, Sam," he says, all friendly just like that time at Trader Joe's.

"I didn't know you were looking to buy a house in the neighborhood."

"I'm not. I'm looking for your mom."

"She's showing a family around the backyard. Would you like a cookie?"

"No, thanks," he says, patting his waistline, which looks pretty thin to me, but what do I know? Soon Mom comes in with a young couple and their five-year-old. The wife really does have a big waistline. I think she's expecting kid number two.

I offer the five-year-old a cookie. He doesn't pat his waistline. The mom and dad each take one and then say, "We'll have our realtor call you," which is always a good sign.

When they leave, I hear Mr. Hill and Mom exchange hellos.

"I didn't know you were looking to buy in the neighborhood, Mr. Hill."

"I'm not. I was looking for you."

Mom offers him a cookie. I could've saved her the trouble.

Then she waves to the young couple with the five-year-old kid as they're getting into their car.

"They seem like a nice family," Mr. Hill says.

"One child and one more on the way," Mom says.

"They ask about the local schools?"

"Everyone asks about the local schools."

"Did you mention our test scores?"

The smile disappears from Mom's face, and you can feel

the temperature dropping in this nice three-bedroom, two-bathroom house.

"There's a banner on the school's fence," Mr. Hill says. "REED MIDDLE SCHOOL. A PLATINUM PERFORMING SCHOOL. Very few schools can boast test scores that high. A badge of honor for the community. It's what house hunters see on their way to an open house."

"A strong selling point," Mom says.

"I'm sure your boss agrees. I hope you'll remember it, Mrs. Warren, when you deposit your next commission. And before your son heads back to court."

I look up at Mom, but she turns away to watch Mr. Hill go.

11

WE BUILD OUR CASE

That article Alistair read about the multitasking brain said people think better while tossing a ball. So on Sunday afternoon at Mr. Kalman's, we toss around a Nerf football, along with ideas on why homework has to go. Sadie takes notes.

"It makes us fat," Alistair says.

"How so?" Sean asks.

"We spend too much time at our desks. We should be outside exercising."

I high-five him for that. Even parents have time for exercise.

Alistair tosses the Nerf to Catalina. "It makes us poor," she says. "All the time we spend doing homework, we could be earning money."

"We're minors, Catalina," Sean says. "The law says we

can't work more than four hours a day while school's in session."

"*Exactly!*" Catalina says. "We *are* working that much. On homework."

Sadie writes down "child labor laws."

Jaesang puts up his hand. Catalina throws him a perfect spiral. "Bad for the economy."

We all look at him like, *Wait, what?*

"Kids doing homework aren't out spending money at the mall."

"Neither are their parents, who have to hire tutors," Sean adds.

Now Sadie puts up her hand, and Jaesang tosses her the ball.

"I forget what it's like to have fun." She looks at Sean. "Really, I can't remember a time when I didn't have this constant feeling like, gotta study, gotta make myself stand out from the crowd."

I put up my hand. She tosses the ball to me.

"Homework takes away my sister time."

Sadie looks at me, and everybody listens. "We used to watch movies together and fight over who got more Pirate's Booty. We'd make stop-motion movies and go to the park with our dogs. We had a life outside of school. Now all that's gone. I mean, we already spend enough time with our teachers during the day. Why do they have to follow us home?"

"You're on to something, Sam," Mr. Kalman says. "The government can't intrude into the private lives of its citizens. It's in the Bill of Rights."

Sadie and Sean bonk their heads as if even the phrase is painful to them.

"The Bill of Rights!"

They jump up and snap to attention like poodles at a dog show. Sean holds out a hand and I pass him the Nerf.

"Congress shall make no law respecting an establishment of religion, or prohibiting the free exercise thereof."

He tosses the ball to Sadie. "Or abridging the freedom of speech."

Who passes it back to Sean. "Or of the press."

Who passes it to Sadie again. "Or the right of the people peaceably to assemble."

Back to Sean. "And to petition the government for a—"

"Redress of grievances!"

Words start streaming out of their mouths like confetti.

Sadie: "A well regulated militia, being necessary to the security of a free state—"

Sean: "The right of the people to keep and bear arms, shall not be infringed."

Sadie: "No soldier shall, in time of peace be quartered in any house, without the consent of the owner, nor in time of war, but in a manner to be prescribed by law."

Sean: "The right of the people to be secure in their—"

Sadie: "Persons, houses, papers, and effects, against unreasonable searches and seizures . . ."

Together: "'Shall not be violated, and no warrants shall issue, but upon probable cause.' Et cetera! Et cetera! Et cetera!" they say, with a triple salute.

Alistair is amazed and starts applauding. The rest of us clap too.

"Miss Benjamin made us memorize the whole thing," Sean says.

"I can't believe I still remember them all," Sadie says.

It's pretty impressive, I guess, but most of it went over my head. I think I know what grievances are, but what does it mean to redress them?

I glance at Mr. Kalman's face. He looks surprised. Not just surprised, but disappointed.

"You *memorized* the Bill of Rights?"

"Part of the torture of eleventh grade," Sean says.

"No discussion? No context?"

"No time, Mr. Kalman. It was AP US History. We memorized, took a matching test, and moved on."

"And that," Mr. Kalman says, "is what's wrong with our schools."

We call out for pizza because, Mr. Kalman says, we'll be working late tonight. Tomorrow we have a filing deadline for our legal brief—an oxymoron, don't you think, to describe a document that's eighty pages long—and Mr. Kalman needs our help to make sure he's covered all the arguments we plan to make next week in court.

So we plow through the pizza and the pages, and nobody wants to be the first to leave. Catalina, Jaesang, and Sean team up on statistics, reading scientific studies on things like anxiety and stress and sleep among kids today, and the number of hours per night they spend on homework, and whether or not homework even helps kids learn. Sean puts all the information into charts that Mr. Kalman can show in court.

Meanwhile, Sadie is helping Mr. Kalman organize the flow of his argument, something she learned how to do in speech and debate, and Alistair and I keep everyone on track. The whiteboard fills up with Sadie's outline, and soon we need someplace easy to post our to-do list, so Alistair whips off his shirt and says, "I took a bath this morning, guys. I'm a clean slate."

A fire in the fireplace keeps him warm.

Around ten, all that's left are pizza crusts and burnt logs. Mr. Kalman checks the last item off Alistair's shoulder and says the brief is ready to be filed. Sean saves a PDF of it to his Dropbox and prints two copies for Mr. Kalman, who likes to do things old school, by hand.

Then Mr. Kalman thanks us for all the *sweat work*.

"Don't let anyone ever call you slackers," he says. "Not after the yeoman's job you've done here today."

It's funny how Mr. Kalman talks, using words as old as he is. I sneak a peek at my dictionary.com app to find out that we performed *in a loyal, valiant, useful, or workman-like manner, especially in situations that involve a great deal of effort or labor.* In other words, we've been busting our butts tonight. And we should be proud.

Sadie and I stay late to help clean up. Mr. Kalman makes tea and brings out a Sara Lee fudge cake from his freezer. We eat straight from the tin.

Then I hear Sadie tell Mr. Kalman that something's been bothering her since the day we had our hearing. She wants to know what Livingston Gulch meant by *whose urine to test.*

"That was just a little dig at me."

"What for?"

"A case I argued once. Before the Supreme Court."

"*You* argued in front of the Supreme Court?" I say.

"Once upon a time, Sam."

"What about?"

"Drug testing in the public schools. Privacy, really. A high school in Oklahoma decided it wasn't fair to test only athletes for drug use. They didn't want to give the football players a bad reputation, football being something of an institution in that state. So they made a new policy—to test anyone who went out for an extracurricular activity. Band. Orchestra. School paper. Debate."

"The least likely crowds to be on drugs," Sadie says.

"Didn't matter. The school wanted to test as many kids as they could. That way the spotlight would be off the football team."

"Who was your client?"

"I represented a young musician. A Korean American girl about your age. She played trumpet in the band and refused to be tested."

"Why? Was she on drugs?"

"As a matter of fact, she was. She took pills to treat her depression. In her community, mental illness of any kind was considered shameful. My client wanted her situation to stay private. She also wanted to keep doing the one thing that brought her joy: playing music for her school."

"The right of the people to be secure in their persons . . . against unreasonable searches . . . shall not be violated . . . but upon probable cause," Sadie says.

Mr. Kalman's whole face lights up. "You didn't just memorize," he says.

"So did you win the case?" I ask.

He's my lawyer, after all. I've got to know his track record.

"The ruling was five to four, Sam. In favor of the school."

"But that's wrong," Sadie says. "It's unfair."

"The Supreme Court is the last hope, Sadie. It isn't always the best."

There's a knock on Mr. Kalman's door and I already know who it's going to be. We've been here since four and it's past ten, and sure enough when I open the door, it's Mom.

"It's late, Mr. Kalman," she says. "The kids need to get to bed."

12

SADIE VERSUS MOM

Here's what Sadie and Mom *usually* fight about:

Clothes.

"You're wearing *that* to a study session?"

"What's wrong with spaghetti straps and jean shorts?"

"I didn't know you were taking anatomy."

Food.

"That's nowhere near enough dinner, Sadie."

"I'll eat a second banana in an hour."

"Empty stomach, empty head."

"Full stomach, sleepy head. Sleepy head, no homework done."

Coffee.

"What's left in the pot is *mine!*"

"Do you have twenty lines of Latin to translate for tomorrow?"

"No."

"Then I get the last sip."

Laundry.

"I am not your maid!"

"I thought you wanted me to wear more clothes."

Sadie's bedroom floor.

"Clean it up! It's a pigsty!"

"What's the difference? I keep the door shut."

"I can't afford to call the exterminator again."

Lately they've had something new to fight about.

"Your English teacher emailed. You're two papers behind."

"I'll do them over the weekend."

We just came inside. Mom is standing at the bottom of the stairs, her arms folded, all stiff like an exclamation point again.

"Sam, go upstairs, brush your teeth, and get to bed."

I follow the first instruction. From my perch on the third step from the top, I hear Mom tell Sadie she got a grade alert on her phone. "You have an F on your last chem lab."

"Those labs take too much of my time right now."

"And your Common App essay? Is that taking too much of your time too?"

"It's not due till January."

"If you don't keep your eye on the ball, Sadie, someone else will catch it."

"What does that even mean?"

"It means I wonder if you've got your priorities straight. Late papers and a last-minute essay won't get you into half the schools on your list."

"Then I'll aim for the other half. It's *my* future. If I'm spending my time the wrong way, it's on me. Not you."

Then Mom says she feels responsible for that future. She feels responsible, she says, to Sadie's mom.

"Don't you think Emily would have pushed you too?"

It gets very quiet on the stairs.

According to Bernice, everybody has a button. Push it, and the fight begins. Families get in fights, she says, not because everybody knows everybody's business. It's because everybody knows everybody's buttons.

Mine is homework, as we all know.

Sadie's is her mom.

She almost never talks about Emily, but I know she thinks about her a lot. On the rare occasions when she leaves her door open and I happen to be walking by, I sometimes see her standing at her dresser and looking through a picture album from when she was zero, one, two, three, four, and five. Not that I've actively peeked at the photo album, but there was one time when she forgot to triple lock her door, and I went in just to be sure there wasn't anything spontaneously alive on the floor, and accidentally I noticed the album.

Emily had long curly hair. In one picture she's standing up in a cable car in San Francisco, holding Sadie's hand, her hair trailing them like a scarf. Dad must've been the photographer. I think they were on vacation, but one thing I notice in the pictures is that Sadie's mom is always dressed like she's ready for work. If I didn't know better, I'd say Mr. Kalman took her shopping too.

I guess it's not surprising that Sadie feels closer to Dad than she does to Mom. Mom would never let it show, but I think it makes her a little sad. Whenever we're out somewhere, the four of us together, like in a movie line or waiting to pay for stuff at Costco, I notice how we fall into the same spots, me next to Mom next to Dad next to Sadie. Or me next to Sadie next to Dad next to Mom. And on special occasions when we go out for dinner, Dad always asks if we can have a booth. He says he likes the coziness of it. And when we get to the table, Mom always says, "Sadie, why don't you slide in next to your dad?"

It's little things like these that make me feel Sadie's mom is here and not here at the same time.

The long silence ends when I hear Mom say, "I'm just trying to be the mother she would have been."

"You can't be the mother she would have been, Jenny. So please don't try."

Four thousand years ago, I'm pretty sure that would have been the end of my big sister's tongue.

Sadie barrels up the stairs. She has to step over me.

"You're supposed to be in bed," she says, and then she *kicks* me. I want to yell *ouch* because that really hurt. But I hold my tongue. I don't want Mom to know I was eavesdropping.

It takes me extra-long to fall asleep. I'm starting to wonder if maybe all this isn't such a great idea. What if, because of me, Sadie doesn't get into a good college? What if, because of me, Mom gets into trouble with her Coldwell Banker boss?

But what if, because of me, seven hundred thousand kids get out of homework jail?

I tap my meditation app. The Guided Meditation slow-breathes me to sleep.

13

BACK TO COURT

This time at the federal courthouse, Judge Otis Wright the Third doesn't keep us waiting. At exactly ten o'clock he walks into his courtroom, and the bailiff says, "All rise. The United States District Court, Los Angeles County, is now in session. Judge Otis Wright the Third presiding."

Everyone stands, and I mean everyone. The courtroom is packed with kids, parents, teachers, and reporters.

Mr. Powell came with our whole class. He made a special request for a field trip today. Mr. Hill signed that special request because he thinks the school board is going to win and that'll prove he was right to suspend me.

Livingston Gulch is there, of course. Mr. Hill is standing next to him.

Otis Wright the Third says, "You may be seated," and we all sit at once, like we're doing the wave at a Dodgers game. "In the matter of *Warren v. Board of Education*, are the plaintiffs prepared to make their opening remarks?"

Mr. Kalman stands. "We are, Your Honor."

"Proceed."

"Your Honor, every home in this country has something called a door. The people on the inside get to close it. Lock it if they want. A burglar can't come through that door. Neither can the police without probable cause. Yet our schools seem to think they have a key to every home in America, and after hours they can come barging in. A dozen sight words for a kindergartener to memorize. Twenty-five math problems for a first-grader to solve. Book reports. Dioramas. And a great white forest of worksheets. What's their probable cause? That homework increases learning? There's no evidence for that claim. In fact, the Cooper Study out of Duke University showed that in high school, too much homework can have a negative effect on learning. In middle school, homework has little or no impact on test scores. And in elementary school, homework made test scores decline."

"Decline?" the judge asks. "Why's that?"

"Because young brains—all brains—need downtime to absorb what they've learned. The only thing homework increases is stress. My client, Sam Warren, is here to represent all the kids in the district, and all their families, who are asking this court to hang a sign on their front doors: NO TRESPASSING. NO MORE HOMEWORK IN OUR HOMES."

Mr. Kalman steps back and sits down. Livingston Gulch raises his hand.

"Yes, Mr. Gulch?"

"Mind if I ask the boy a question?"

"Go ahead."

Gulch leans in close to me. I can smell the spearmint gum he spat out on his way into court. Plus the In-N-Out Double-Double he had for breakfast. He screws up one eye at me and says, "What level are you up to on Martian Battle Craft?"

"Master Guardian."

He looks away from me to the crowd. "He must not be doing that much homework. I don't know about you, but I've tried that game. Can't get past Junior Cadet myself."

Laughter rumbles from Mr. Hill's side of the courtroom.

I feel myself turning bright red.

"I play the game to get my energy out," I say.

"What's that, son?" Judge Otis Wright the Third asks.

"It's a *may-do*. After my *must-do*s get done. Playing video games helps me feel better. If I didn't have so much homework, I probably wouldn't need to play them that often. And I'd be stuck at Junior Cadet. Like him."

This time all the laughter comes from the kids' side of the room.

I'm expecting the judge to pound his gavel for *order in the court*, but it's Gulch's raised hand that quiets everyone down.

"Yes, Mr. Gulch?" Judge Otis Wright the Third says.

"De minimis non curat lex."

The court is silent. Even Judge Wright is speechless.

"The law," Gulch translates, "does not concern itself with trifles."

"Are you suggesting it was wrong of me to hear this case?"

"No, Judge Wright, I am not. But if this delicate boy needs his downtime more than the rest of us, he should apply for a 504 Education Plan. It's how the district accommodates a child with a learning disability identified by the law. But to aim his arrow at the institution of homework is to waste the time of this fine court. What's more, the research I saw suggests that homework is helpful."

He pulls an index card from his shirt pocket and puts on his reading glasses. "Consider this from Harvard University: 'High schoolers who do their homework earn GPAs that are thirty percent higher than those who don't. Middle schools that give one to two hours per night have higher test scores than the low-achieving schools that don't.' The only reasonable conclusion: homework helps kids learn."

"Objection!" Sadie shouts, jumping to her feet. Which is pretty funny if you consider that she's never been to law school. "Mr. Gulch is misinterpreting those studies."

"Who's she?" Gulch asks.

"My legal assistant," Mr. Kalman says.

"Qualifications?"

Sean springs up.

"Captain of the debate team. Winner of six Lincoln-Douglas awards and over ninety speaker points at the state finals."

Otis Wright the Third tells Sadie to "proceed."

"Thank you, Your Honor," she says. "Mr. Gulch has a flaw in his logic. First of all, the higher grade point average among students who do their homework might only prove that by doing their homework, they please their teachers, who reward them with higher grades. It doesn't necessarily mean they're learning anything."

"What about the test scores?"

"There may be a *correlation* between heavy homework and high test scores, but that doesn't mean there's a *cause*. The test scores might be higher because the level of education in the homes is higher. Or they might be higher because the teachers are teaching to the test. Or worse, cheating on it to boost kids' scores. To prove there's a cause, you'd have to take one class of students and randomly split them into two groups—one gets a lot of homework, the other gets none. Then see which group has higher scores. My guess is it would be the one that gets none."

"Really?" Gulch says. "Let us ask someone with perfect standardized test scores. If it pleases the court, we'll hear now from Cindy Vale."

A perky middle-schooler in plaid comes up the aisle carrying a covered tray, like a waitress at a five-star restaurant.

"Tell the court, Cindy, if you would, how much homework you get per night."

"Honestly, I can't speak for all the other kids, but I spend, oh, maybe, two hours. A little more on Mondays because I believe in getting a head start."

"Does the homework cause you any stress?"

"Not at all. In fact, I know some kids will laugh at me for this, but I like homework. I appreciate the extended learning opportunities it provides, like in this project we were asked to do."

She lifts the cover off her tray. "A 3-D biorama."

We all lean forward to behold a display board with 3-D trees, text, drawings, and birds. It looks like a page from a life-size pop-up book.

"What's a biorama?" Judge Wright asks.

"It's a biographical diorama. Or a dioramic biography. I did mine on John James Audubon. The teacher asked us to go above and beyond this time. So I added a feature of my own invention. Robotic birds."

Next thing we know, these animatronic arctic terns, American magpies, and tricolor herons take off from her posterboard and start soaring around the courtroom, while an American flamingo steps onto the judge's desk.

There are gasps and *oooh*s and *aah*s and *whoa*s coming at us from every side.

Behind me I hear Sean tell Sadie, "We should've hired her."

"Your Honor," Cindy Vale says, "if you abolish home-work, students like me who are hungry for more challenge will get bored. And I'm afraid we'll fall even further behind other countries. Like China."

Her birds all come back to roost. She beams a perfect teacher's-pet smile at Livingston Gulch.

But Catalina notices something and leaps up.

"Look at her fun facts!"

The judge turns to look at the biorama.

"What about them?"

"Fun fact number five: 'Adopted by Captain Jean and Anne Audubon, John James was given a good education and plenty of leisure time. This extra time made him notice his own curiosity in the nature around him.' That's because he didn't grow up with a ton of homework!"

"Thank you, Catalina," Mr. Kalman says, "that's exactly our point. Your Honor, we aren't suggesting that homework be eliminated so that children can be bored. We're saying the students and their families should have the freedom to choose how they spend their time outside of school. Sam, if you didn't have homework in the afternoons, what would you do?"

"I'd play piano. Walk my dogs. Build a treehouse with my dad."

"And you, Sadie?"

"I'd volunteer at a legal clinic. Start reading for pleasure again and spend time with my little brother."

He calls to the kids' half of the courtroom. "What about the rest of you?"

One by one, kids start to answer him.

"I'd bake with my grandma."

"I'd train my parrot."

"I'd train my voice."

"I'd post more comics on iFunny."

"I'd babysit."

"Build an app."

"Teach art to younger children."

"Learn a thousand digits of pi."

"Go to Laker Camp."

"Try out for *MasterChef Junior*."

"I would do nothing," Sean says. "And in doing nothing, I would discover what to do."

"Your Honor, if homework is the wall standing between these children and their dreams, maybe it's time to tear it down."

It's supposed to be quiet inside a courtroom, but right now it sounds like a gym—and we just hit a buzzer shot for three.

Outside we're greeted by a crowd of people exercising their First Amendment right to assemble. I've been in crowds before, like at Disneyland waiting to get on Space Mountain, or in the seats at Staples Center. But I've never been in a crowd that's there because of me.

Kids I don't even know come up to say hi. They tell me that even if we lose, they think it's awesome that I tried.

That feels great. That makes me proud.

And I go on shaking, fist bumping, and high-fiving kid hand after kid hand, until one of the hands is suddenly twice as big.

It's Mr. Powell. "You've shown a lot of courage, Sam," he says.

Then he turns to Mr. Kalman. "We're not all monsters, you know. Teachers don't necessarily want to be assigning so much homework."

"Why do you, then?"

"Because the district is broke. They cut the school year but not the curriculum. They cram so many kids into our classes, we can't get everything done between eight and three. And because they tie our jobs, our raises, and our retirement to the test scores."

If you're a teacher these days, you get ranked just like an athlete. Only it's not *your* stats they rank you by, but your students' stats. Their test scores. I guess it makes sense. How do you know if a teacher is good? Look at his students' test scores. But I've spent a lot of time in classrooms, and I can tell you that some kids are so bored, they can hardly stay awake. And some can hardly stay awake because they were up too late the night before. Doing home-work.

"That may be unfair," Mr. Kalman says. "It may even be illegal. That's for other courts to decide. But we shouldn't be taking it out on kids."

A reporter for the *LA Times* wants to know how we think we did. I don't really know how we did. It's that same feeling you have right after a test. I guess we did okay, but we have to wait for the results.

Then Mr. Kalman comes face-to-face with Mom.

"Did I convince you?" he asks.

Mom thinks for a minute. Then she says, "I still believe kids need to do their homework to compete. But while I might not agree with the message, I've never seen my children work so hard for anything."

She means we did a yeoman's job. Maybe, for now, that's all that matters.

14

A NEW FACE
ON THE SIGN

We spend the rest of the day hanging around the courthouse, waiting for the judge's decision.

Around three o'clock, word comes that he won't decide until tomorrow at the earliest. So we all go home.

We're driving into our neighborhood when I see that house for sale, the one where I gave out fresh-baked cookies to the young couple with one kid and another on the way. Only something's different about that house. Not the house, but the sign out front.

There's no picture of Mom. Instead there's a picture of another real estate agent in Mom's office. A man with a mustache named Tim O'Riley.

"Mom," I say, "what happened to your picture?"

She glances at Tim O'Riley's face as we go by.

"I'm no longer the agent for that house, honey."

"Why not?"

"I don't work for the company anymore."

"What do you mean? You won top sales five years in a row."

"Well, someone else can win it next year."

The car is quiet as we pass the school and turn onto Otsego Street. It's quiet as we pull into the garage. Everyone gets out except for me and Mom.

"Did you lose your job because of me?"

"No, Sam. I lost my job because I had a disagreement with my boss."

"Over what?"

"He thinks that the lawsuit is bad for business."

I feel like Livingston Gulch slithered into the car.

After dinner that night, I don't just clear the dinner dishes; I *put them in the dishwasher.* And I wipe the table, take out the trash, and make the next day's lunches for Sadie and me. I even cut the crust off my almond butter and Nutella sandwich because that's how Mom does it.

Then I fill a bucket with sudsy water.

"What are you doing, Sam?" Mom asks.

"Getting ready to wash your car."

"Honey, it's almost your bedtime."

"I know."

"My car's not that dirty."

"I saw a few smudges."

"Really, it's nothing I can't wipe clean tomorrow."

"Better if I wipe it clean tonight."

She puts a hand on my shoulder. She's a mom and knows what's up. "Sam, it's not your fault I lost my job."

"You said so yourself. Your boss thinks the lawsuit is bad for business. That means you got fired because of me."

I carry the bucket the rest of the way into the garage.

Later, on my way to bed, I stop by Sadie's door and ignore the sign.

"Sadie," I say, knocking loud this time, "can I come in?"

She doesn't say no.

I push open the door, go in, and sit on her bed. There are too many dishes and too much laundry for me to sit on the floor.

"You did great today," I say. "What you said about correlation being different from cause. Even I understood."

"Thanks, Sam."

"I'll bet you get it from your mom." She looks at me. "She was a lawyer, right?"

She nods.

"I think about her sometimes," I say. "About meeting her. I know that's impossible because if I could meet your mom, Dad never would have met Jenny and then I never would've been born. But still . . . I wish I could meet her."

"You can meet her, Sam."

Sadie gets real quiet for a second. She looks at me as if she's trying to decide something.

"Close your eyes," she says.

I close my eyes and hear Sadie's floor creak as she walks across it. Then I hear a sound and I guess she's taking a book from her shelf. I hear pages flipping and then Sadie's voice.

"Okay, you can open your eyes."

I do, and I see she's holding a piece of paper in her hands.

"She wrote me a letter every year on my birthday," Sadie says. "This is the last one I got. You can get to know her a little from this." She reads it aloud.

DEAR SADIE. TODAY YOU TURN FIVE; FIVE IS A JUMPING-OFF NUMBER. SEE THE LEDGE ON TOP? FROM THE TOP OF FIVE YOU LEAP INTO THE NEXT PART OF YOUR LIFE. INTO KINDERGARTEN. TYING YOUR OWN SHOES. AND LEARNING HOW TO READ. AND ONCE YOU CAN READ, YOU GET TO LIVE MANY LIVES AT ONCE. YOURS AND ALL THE WONDERFUL LIVES IN STORIES. BUT BEFORE YOU LEAP INTO FIVE, HERE'S A MEMORY I HAVE OF YOU WHEN YOU WERE TWO. IT'S OF YOUR FAVORITE GAME.

AT THE PARK, WE USED TO PLAY HOW HIGH? I WOULD PUT YOU IN THE SWING AND PUSH YOU

UP, JUST A LITTLE, AND ASK, "HOW HIGH DO YOU
WANT TO GO, SADIE?" AND YOU'D SAY, "HIGHER."
SO I'D PUSH YOU UP A LITTLE MORE.

"THIS HIGH?" I'D SAY.

"HIGHER!"

I'D LIFT THE SWING SOME MORE.

"THIS HIGH?"

"HIGHER!"

I'D HOIST YOU SO HIGH IN THAT SWING THAT
YOUR DROOL WOULD DRIP ON MY FOREHEAD.

THEN I'D LET GO. YOU WOULD FLY THROUGH
THE AIR SQUEALING AND KICKING. THE WHOLE
SWING SET SHOOK WITH YOUR LAUGHTER.

"AGAIN!" YOU'D SAY.

REMEMBER, SADIE BELLE, THERE'S A SPIRIT
INSIDE YOU THAT WANTS TO FLY HIGH.

LOVE,

MOMMY.

Sadie turns the letter around for me to see her mom's
handwriting. Then she folds it up and tells me to close my
eyes so she can put it away.

When I'm allowed to open them again, I realize

something and say, "Both moms are telling you the same thing."

"What do you mean?"

"Your mom and ours. They both want you to fly high."

I have a hard time falling asleep again. I think about Mom losing her job and how that must feel. Maybe if we lose the case, her boss will ask her to come back and she can get top sales again. I think about Sadie fighting with her and how that must feel. What if she's right? Sadie's been too distracted by the case to focus on what really matters right now, which is college.

Then my thoughts go to Judge Otis Wright the Third, and I wonder how all this is sitting on his mind. Mr. Kalman says a judge has probably the hardest job in the world, harder even than a referee, because there's the right thing to do, and there's the legal thing to do, but they aren't always the same.

Is that a paradox? The right and wrong of it, side by side in one decision?

It occurs to me that if Judge Otis Wright the Third is lying in his bed right now, trying to fall asleep, and I'm lying in mine, maybe we're on the same thought channel and I can send him a mental message.

So from my pillow to his, this is what I send: *Hello there,*

Judge Otis Wright the Third. Sam Warren here. I just want you to know that it's okay if you decide the case against me.

I sure hope the other seven hundred thousand kids in the district didn't hear that.

Tuesday morning we're sitting in Mr. Powell's class doing a worksheet on decimals when Miss Lochman comes in to say, "Sam, Alistair, Jaesang, and Catalina, get your backpacks and come with me."

We look at one another like four criminals suddenly caught, only I can't remember doing anything wrong since I held up my NO HOMEWORK sign. I get this twisty, queasy feeling as we follow Miss Lochman out the door.

"Where are you taking us?" Alistair asks.

"To the front gate. You're being pulled out of school."

"What for? What'd we do?"

"I was just told to come get you."

She escorts us down the hall, down the stairs, and out the double doors into the yard. There's a cold wind blowing dead leaves up from the ground, back into the trees. A worried wind. My stomach starts to flip, but when I see who's standing on the other side of the gate waiting for us, it lands again.

"Dad?" I say.

"He's made a decision."

"Who?"

"Judge Wright. Mr. Kalman called. Said to get you down to the courthouse right away. We have twenty minutes to get there."

We hop on the freeway and race downtown in the carpool lane. We park and come up to the street level and find Sadie and Sean in front, waiting for us with Mr. Kalman. We all go in together and head up to room 527.

The minute the door to the judge's chambers opens, we all stand.

Judge Otis Wright the Third asks us to "sit, please," and we do.

Then he sits in his tall leather chair and opens a folder. He takes out a single sheet of paper. He looks right at me for a second. Then his eyes drift down to the paper. He reads it aloud.

"If this were a case of one individual seeking injunctive relief from the stresses of homework, I could find in favor of the plaintiff. But I don't believe you have made a strong enough case for damages to the entire class. Nor do I find the privacy argument compelling enough to outweigh the district's urgent obligation to educate the children. Therefore, in the matter of *Warren v. Board of Education*, I find in favor of the district. The claim is denied."

"What's it mean?" Alistair asks.

Sadie turns to me. "You follow that?"

"Yeah," I say. "We lost."

Outside the courtroom we're ambushed by a mob of reporters. One shoves a microphone in my face.

"Sam," he says as if he knows me, "how do you feel about today's verdict?"

"Lousy."

"Are you going to appeal to the Ninth Circuit?"

I hadn't thought about this. If you sue in federal court and lose, you can ask a higher court for a second chance.

I look at Sadie and shrug. From a few steps up, a voice booms down.

"You bet your ass we're going to appeal," Mr. Kalman says.

15

SAM FRANCISCO

Who would've thought that standing on a desk could lead to sitting on a plane? Three weeks later we fly to San Francisco to go before the Ninth Circuit Court of Appeals.

It almost didn't happen. When Mr. Kalman found out it would take 180 days and Alistair finger-counted all the way to summer, we practically gave up. Mr. Kalman said he wasn't sure he would even live that long. And we couldn't appeal without our lawyer.

Catalina calculated our odds of winning the appeal at a hundred to one against, so we were all willing to let it go.

Not Sadie. "There's got to be a way we can move to the front of the line," she said.

Sean suggested a hunger strike because that's what Gandhi would have done.

"Only as a last resort, please," said Alistair.

Then I remembered learning about Rosa Parks, how she was tired after a long day at work and refused to give up her seat on the bus for a white passenger. The bus driver said, "I'll have you arrested," and Rosa Parks said, "You may have me arrested." And then Martin Luther King Jr. and another minister named Ralph Abernathy organized a boycott of the buses in Montgomery. "Don't ride the bus," they said. And the people all told their friends, "Don't ride the bus."

"For a long time almost no black people, and not very many white people, rode the bus," I told Sadie and Sean, Alistair, Jaesang, Catalina, and Mr. Kalman. "That's what got the attention of the Supreme Court. And in 1956 they ruled you can't separate people based on the color of their skin. So by sitting down, Rosa Parks stood up for her rights."

Which is a paradox, if you think about it.

"Just like you, Sam!" Alistair said. "Only you stood up to stand up for our rights."

"Boycott," Sean said. "Brilliant. We stop going to school until the appeals court takes our case."

We all looked at Mr. Kalman.

"It's bold," he said. "But if you incite a boycott of the schools, you could get suspended."

"Wouldn't be the first time," I said.

"I suppose if you got enough kids all over the state to stay home, just for a few days . . . the appeals court would notice." Then he turned to Sean and said, "It's time for a new video on the Interweb."

We went to work on a new video urging kids to stay home.

"Don't get out of bed.

"Don't get on the bus.

"Don't set foot in school.

"Until our appeal to stop homework gets heard."

The video went viral. The next day, forty thousand kids stayed home. The day after that, three hundred thousand more. By Thursday, 90 percent of all public school kids in California had the "flu." The state superintendent made a phone call.

Not to the Centers for Disease Control in Atlanta.

Not to Mr. Kalman.

Not to me.

Not to the governor.

He called the clerk at the Ninth Circuit Court of Appeals. He begged him to put us on the docket right away.

And that's how our case got to the front of the line.

On the plane to San Francisco, Alistair asks the flight attendant for a napkin. Then he asks her for a pen. Then he asks me for my autograph because he thinks our homework case is going to make me famous.

"Shut up," I say.

"No, really. The boy who took on homework. I want your autograph while you're still flying coach."

"I am not autographing a napkin for you, Alistair," I say. "You'll use it to wipe Sriracha from your face."

"Okay," he says, "then sign this."

He lifts his shirt. "Make the bellybutton the *a* in *Sam*."

He holds the pen out to me, but I don't take it. I don't want to jinx our case.

"Tell you what," I say. "I'll give you my autograph if we win."

Alistair puts the napkin on his tray but pockets the pen.

Behind us, through the crack made by Alistair's fully reclined seat, I can hear the sweet whisperings of Sadie and Sean. He's quizzing her on her SAT vocab.

"Clandestine."

"Secretive."

"Exonerate."

"Free from guilt."

"Neophyte."

"Beginner."

"Inveigh."

"Protest."

"Surfeit."

"Excess."

"Kiss me."

"On a plane?"

Then it goes quiet.

Across the aisle, Jaesang and Catalina are thumb wrestling. Alistair flips through the in-flight magazine, tearing out restaurant reviews and recipes. Meanwhile, Mr. Kalman reads the *LA Times*. I see him fold it over, then fold it over again, then fold it a third time, as if he's trying to make a giant paper football, which is odd because Mr. Kalman doesn't seem like a paper football kind of guy. But when it's one-eighth of its original size, he leans over and hands it to me. His bony finger taps a headline:

NINTH CIRCUIT TO HEAR BOY'S PLEA FOR HOMEWORK HELP

I read the article and when I get to my name, it feels like there's a hummingbird trapped in my stomach: *Eleven-year-old Sam Warren was suspended for refusing to do homework over the Columbus Day holiday.*

A few sentences later, it says: *His attorney, Mr. Avi Kalman, is no neophyte*—hey, I know that word!—*to constitutional law. A longtime advocate of children's rights, Mr. Kalman argued for the plaintiff in* Lee v. Oklahoma School District *before the US Supreme Court.*

I look over at Mr. Kalman. I know he wanted me to see my name in the paper, and that's why he folded it up for me, but I'm glad I saw the part about him, too.

"Mr. Kalman," I say after folding up the article. "I was thinking about what the judge said, how if it had been just me suing and not the whole class, he might've ruled with us. We need to find a way to show that homework is bad for all kids, not just one."

"What do you have in mind?"

"Backpacks."

"Backpacks?"

"We should weigh them. Not just ours, but all of them. If we got kids across the country to weigh their backpacks and we kept a running total on the website, that could be a pretty huge number."

"I like the way you're thinking, Sam. Like an attorney. We'll have Sean add it to the site."

When we land in San Francisco, Mr. Kalman tells the cab driver, "The Ninth Circuit Court of Appeals, please."

That's all he has to say. He doesn't have to give an address because every cab driver in the city knows where the Ninth Circuit Court of Appeals is. On the way, Mr. Kalman tells us about some of the famous cases that were heard there.

One was a lawsuit brought by Vanna White of *Wheel of Fortune*. An electronics company made an ad that had a robot turning over letters the way Vanna White does. She thought they were making fun of her, or worse — copying her. "It's not fair if they make money off the thing I made famous," she said.

The Ninth Circuit Court of Appeals agreed with Vanna White. The robot had to stop turning over letters.

Should the police be allowed to slap a GPS tracking device on a suspect's car, then watch where it goes, even if they don't have a warrant?

The Ninth Circuit said yes, they can. Following a suspect isn't the same as searching them.

The cout also said that California's Proposition 8 banning gay marriage was unconstitutional. The Equal Protection Clause says you should be able to marry the person you love, even if they are the same sex as you.

The other side appealed to the US Supreme Court. The Supreme Court upheld the Ninth Circuit's decision. Now everybody who wants to, gay or straight, can marry.

And when the president tried to stop people from just seven countries from entering the US, the Ninth Circuit said no, you can't do that. Not without proving why those countries' citizens are a greater threat than all the other countries' citizens.

So the Ninth Circuit Court of Appeals decides some big issues. Their next big issue: homework.

We get out of the cab and have to make our way through a crowd. It's mostly kids playing hooky on a Monday and holding up signs that read:

STOP HOMEWORK NOW.

SAVE OUR CHILDHOOD.

WELCOME TO *SAM* FRANCISCO.

That last one makes me smile.

Inside, it's a crowded courtroom like last time, only now Mr. Kalman and Livingston Gulch go at it in front of three judges instead of one.

Mr. Kalman leads with the child labor argument. You might not know this, but in the old days — we're talking before the 1900s — kids didn't have to go to school. They went to work instead. Farm work. Factory work. Or as helpers, called apprentices, in a trade. Some people took advantage of the kids, making them work twelve-hour days and paying them way less than they would adults. Congress passed a law to stop this.

"The Fair Labor Standards Act prohibits minors under fourteen from working more than four hours a day while school is in session. Yet millions of children are doing just that on homework."

"The child labor laws apply only to minors who work for other people," Gulch says. "Kids doing homework are working for themselves. For their own benefit."

"Moreover," Mr. Kalman continues, "pediatricians are recommending that children between the ages of five and ten get ten hours of sleep per night. Teenagers should be getting nine and a quarter."

It was Sean's idea to bring up the health angle. He did all this research on the brain and found out that most teenagers are getting between six and seven hours of sleep a night, which, if you ask me, accounts for their nasty moods at dinnertime.

"So sue for naptime in the high schools," Gulch says. "But don't get rid of homework."

Mr. Kalman tries the Fourteenth Amendment argument. "When learning takes place in school, students have equal access to the teacher. When you send work home, learning becomes separate and unequal. Rich kids get tutors and technology. The poor struggle on their own."

Alistair, Jaesang, Catalina, and I do fist bumps in our seats.

Livingston Gulch raises his hand.

"Yes, Mr. Gulch?"

"Two kids attend the same school," he says. "One arrives with lunch from home: grilled salmon with miso sauce and a side of lobster sushi. The other is on the district's lunch program: a burrito and a packet of hot sauce. By no measure is that fair. But our schools are here to educate children, not equalize them."

Mr. Kalman holds up a bar graph. "I have here a copy of a graph from the CDC that we submitted. It shows the number of ADHD and GAD diagnoses among school-age children between 2003 and 2017. The CDC report shows a steady increase of five percent a year."

Jaesang and Catalina fist bump each other. They found those statistics!

Mr. Kalman pulls a second graph from his briefcase. "And this chart shows the average amount of homework done per night, from the updated Cooper Study completed just this year. Note the same five percent a year increase in the number of minutes per night students at all levels are spending on homework. Side by side, these charts tell the story of the growing pressure we put on children and its impact on their mental health."

There's a long silence in the courtroom. The three judges on the Ninth Circuit Court of Appeals wait patiently while Gulch thinks of something to say.

And for a minute I feel like this is it. We've won. What can he possibly say to that? The more homework kids get, the more stressed they are. It's right there in those two charts.

But just as a cobra's head comes up when it's about to strike, here comes Gulch's hand.

"Your Honors," he says, glancing at Sadie, "if I may suggest a flaw in my opponent's logic. There may be a *correlation* between the increase in homework and the spike in ADHD and anxiety diagnoses among school-age children, but as any high school debater will tell you, that does not mean there's a *cause*. Perhaps school has grown more stressful because there's more to learn in each precious day. All the more reason why we shouldn't constrain our teachers by telling them not to give homework."

"We have testimony from over thirty thousand school-age children—" Mr. Kalman starts to say.

But one of the judges interrupts with, "If they had so much homework, when did they find the time to complain?"

I can see Mr. Kalman starting to wear out. I look at Sadie. She's worried.

Another judge asks, "And what's the constitutional violation?"

"The constitutional violation? Well, Your Honors, in *Griswold* the court established the sanctity of the bedroom. The same exclusion of the government from our nation's living rooms, dining rooms, and kids' rooms has to be applied. After four it's family time."

Mr. Kalman is talking about *Griswold v. Connecticut,* a case we looked up on PocketJustice. It's this cool app Sean showed us on his iPad. You can search any Supreme Court decision and read a transcript of the case. You can even listen to an audio of the arguments.

Griswold was about privacy—that married people should be able to do whatever they want behind closed doors. The court ruled that just as the Fourth Amendment won't let the government search our homes without a reason, it won't let them tell us what we can and can't do inside those homes. Mr. Kalman is trying to show that by giving homework, schools are crossing the line that the Fourth Amendment draws at our front doors.

But Livingston Gulch points to another case, *Pierce v. Society of Sisters,* in which the right to educate children belongs to the states, not the federal government. It's the same argument he raised the first time we went to court.

Mr. Kalman tries bringing up *Brown v. Board of Education* to prove that some school-related cases *do* belong in federal court.

One thing I notice is there's a Supreme Court case for just about everything, and you'd better know them all if you want to score points.

After about twenty more minutes of arguments, the justices of the Ninth Circuit Court of Appeals signal that time is up. Then they announce that they'll be going directly into conference. There are too many kids whose lives are affected by this decision. A swift ruling is the best way to restore order in the schools.

I couldn't agree more—especially if they side with us.

16

BEST SUNDAE EVER

We're due back in court at two o'clock. Alistair says we should "leave the lunch plans" to him. We go outside and hop on a cable car headed for Fisherman's Wharf. The ride is windy and cold and we all huddle together, but we're laughing because riding in a cable car in San Francisco is a blast. It's somewhere between flying and riding a bike, but better because you're defying gravity while on the ground. Wait a minute . . . how can you defy gravity *on the ground?* Weird, but on a cable car that's how it feels.

"I love this city," Sean says.

We're holding on to the same pole, leaning out into the cold wind.

"Me too," I say.

"If I play my cards right, I'll be back in the Bay Area next year for college."

"How so?"

"Well, Sam, I'm applying to UC Berkeley. They've got a city planning program that I really want to do. If I can keep my grades down, I might have a shot."

"You mean, if you can keep your grades up."

"No. Down. I'm on the Academic Decathlon team. It has to have at least three C students, and I'm one of the three. If I start getting Bs or As, I could get kicked off the team. And the team is the best thing I've got going for my college app. I've always struggled with school. My SATs will never get me in. But my C average just might."

Okay, so a C average is the only way for Sean to get into Berkeley. If that's not a paradox, I don't know what is.

At Fisherman's Wharf, we eat fish and chips on the docks and then walk over to Ghirardelli Square for what Alistair promises will be the world's best hot fudge sundae. Ever.

We stand looking up at the enormous lights spelling out G-h-i-r-a-r-d-e-l-l-i. The air smells like salt from the sea, plus churros from a cart, plus scented candles from a store, plus fish from everywhere.

But near the Ghirardelli sign, all those other smells bow down to chocolate. Milk chocolate, mint chocolate, dark chocolate, white chocolate (which, according to the posters, isn't even chocolate at all).

After a long wait that feels longer the closer we get to that chocolate source, we're seated at a big booth, and not too long after that we're digging through clouds of whipped cream, thick hot fudge, and crunchy chopped peanuts to sweet cold ice cream in giant glass bowls.

Sean and Catalina are sharing.

Jaesang and Mr. Kalman are sharing.

Me and Sadie are sharing.

Alistair and Alistair are sharing.

"Man," he says, "isn't this the best hot fudge sundae you ever had?"

We all nod. Except for Sadie, who says, "I've been here before."

"You have?" I say, because *I* never have.

"My mom brought me, Sam, the year she died. We came to San Francisco because she wanted to show me where she grew up. We ordered hot fudge sundaes and she said, 'This is the best hot fudge sundae you'll ever have.'"

We all watch as Sadie takes a slow bite, and Sean slips his arm through hers.

At two o'clock we're back in court. The judges come out of their chambers, and the senior justice of the three delivers the ruling.

"This case requires that we consider whether the routine practice of assigning homework to K-twelve students violates the constitutional rights accorded to families and minors under the Fourth and Fourteenth Amendments. Sam Warren, a sixth-grader, was suspended from Reed Middle

School for refusing to write down a homework assignment and for standing on a desk as he urged his fellow students to do the same. He later filed a claim for damages against the district, alleging psychological distress. The claim was rejected, and Attorney Avi Kalman filed suit as next friend in federal court. Due to the number of students in the district who could make the same claim, class action status was granted.

"The district court denied the plaintiff's claim. We received it on appeal.

"Having listened carefully to both sides, we find that the plaintiff has not adequately proved material damages to himself or to members of the class. We therefore unanimously affirm the lower court's denial of claim. In addition, we grant the appellee's request to impose the maximum allowable fine of ten thousand dollars under the California False Claims Act."

In other words, we lost again.

Not only that, but we owe ten grand to Livingston Gulch!

Outside, I hear a scraping sound. It's the wooden stakes that held the signs. They're being dragged along the sidewalk as all the people walk away. I glance over and see WELCOME TO *SAM* FRANCISCO getting smaller. It doesn't feel good to see my name upside down.

A journalist shoves his microphone at Mr. Kalman. I've never understood that. If they really want you to talk to them, shouldn't they invent a smaller recording device so it doesn't seem like they're pulling out a weapon?

"What do you say to another appeal, Mr. Kalman? Are you going to take homework all the way to the Supreme Court?"

Mr. Kalman looks at all our disappointed faces.

"I don't know," he says. "We'll have to see."

He walks past us to the street, then raises his hand for a cab. His hand goes up slowly, like someone who's not sure he has the right answer.

17

COFFEE AND CANDLELIGHT

The kids at school treat me like the boy whose dog died. All sympathy all the time. At handball, if I get out on a clean slicey, somebody calls "blockies" and I get a second chance. If there's a line at the cafeteria, I get moved to the front. After school, girls in seventh grade come up to me and offer to carry my backpack. It's nice and all, but what I really want is to be treated like a normal kid.

Mr. Hill *is* treating me like a normal kid. Thursday at recess I sneak into the multi-purpose room. I sit at the piano and am about to play when he leans in and says, "I'm sorry, Sam, but the piano is reserved for students who will be in the winter program."

At lunch the Fab Four land at our regular table. Jaesang pulls out his tray of Korean sushi, and Catalina unwraps a burrito. Then they trade.

I have my same old peanut butter and Nutella sandwich.

Alistair's lunch usually starts with him spreading a cloth napkin on the table, taking the lids off various Tupperwares, and "plating" a meal of fabulous leftovers he cooked the night before. Today he unwraps —

"A *PB and J?* Where's my friend Alistair, and what have you done with him?"

"I didn't feel like cooking last night, Sam. Now that we lost the case, I've lost my appetite for fine food."

He crunches a celery stick. I take a bite of my soggy sandwich and think, *What have I done?*

And to make things even worse, my teachers all assigned *un montón* of homework, due tomorrow.

In the afternoon when I walk home, I notice Mr. Kalman's *LA Times* still sitting in the gutter. I pick it up and walk it to his front door. On the porch I look through the window and see a candle burning. It's one of those tall, fat candles in a glass holder with Hebrew letters on it. Last year around this time he lit one too, but I don't know why.

I knock on his door. No answer. I ring the bell. No answer. I leave the paper on the porch.

At home, we eat dinner together. Even Sadie's been eating with us every night since we lost in San Francisco. I ask Mom if she found a new job yet and she says, "Not yet, but I'll keep looking."

After dinner, in the living room, Sadie sits on the couch opposite Dad, their socks touching, feet to feet. He watches

Thursday Night Football while she works on her Common App essay.

I know I'm not supposed to look over her shoulder, but I'm curious to see what she's writing about, so I pretend to be sweeping the floor.

"What are you doing, Sam?" she asks.

"Sweeping the floor."

"Since when?"

"I ate a cookie in the general vicinity of the couch. Probably dropped some crumbs."

I sweep around the back of the couch and peek at her yellow pad. The title of her essay is "My Greatest Failure."

Halfway down the first paragraph I see the words "my brother" and "lawsuit."

Bernice says failure is the greenhouse of success. Right now it feels more like the doghouse.

Or the outhouse.

I want to say something, but I'm not allowed to because I'm only sweeping, not snooping. I don't want Sadie to feel like she's done anything wrong. The loss is my greatest failure, not hers. In Prisoner when you yell "Jailbreak!" and then drop the ball, whose fault is that?

Later, I hoist my backpack into my bedroom. I have math review exercises, notes on a science chapter, chapter 12 of

Black Ships Before Troy to read, and a current event due because I missed Monday to be in *San* Francisco.

At my desk, I flick on the light and start my work. I'm my big sister's greatest failure, so I decide that from now on, I'm going to work hard and get good grades and make her proud. Besides, we lost. We gave it our best shot. It's time to get my priorities straight.

I wake up in a puddle of my own drool. It's still dark out. Across the street I see candlelight flickering in Mr. Kalman's window. My cell phone tells me it's 3:35 in the morning. Plenty of time to get things done.

Eight scoops. That's what I remember Mom counting out every morning when she makes her coffee. Eight scoops and water to the ten-cup line. Or is it ten scoops and water to the eight-cup line? Yeah, that sounds more like it.

I wait for the coffeemaker to gurgle and hiss, and that's how I know it's ready. I reach for a mug, see that it's Mom's Coldwell Banker top sales mug, and put it back. I'm still mad at the company, so I take an ordinary white one instead.

To tell you the truth, I've never tasted coffee before. Everyone says it's a required taste. Required for what, I always wondered. Now I know.

Mom drinks hers black. Dad loads his up with cream and sugar. And Sadie puts soymilk in hers. With enough milk and sugar, anything goes down easy. And once it's down, I'll be up and ready to work.

Ready to show my teachers that I'm not a slacker, not a lazy complainer who lost his lawsuit. Ready to show them all that I can get back on their field and win.

I hold the mug to my lips and blow. Even with cream and sugar, this smells gross.

"What are you doing?"

I spin around. Sadie is standing in the kitchen doorway, holding her laptop and a stack of books. She eyes the mug of coffee in my hand.

"Since when do *you* drink coffee in the middle of the night?"

"I've got five things due in four hours."

I take a long, sweet, milky, *and* bitter sip. Sadie sets down her laptop and her books and charges over.

"Give me that."

"No."

She grabs my arm.

"No way an eleven-year-old is going to get jacked up on caffeine just to do his homework."

"Why not? You do it all the time."

"I'm practically an adult."

She starts to twist.

I resist.

She twists harder.

I let go.

She dumps the coffee into the sink.

I reach for the pot and pull it off the warming plate.

"I can drink it straight from the pot," I say.

She grabs my arm again and pries two of my fingers off the handle. The other two and my thumb stay put.

"Sam, let go of the pot."

"Make your own," I snap.

She gives a tug.

I tug back.

She jerks.

I jerk back.

Then she pretends to give up, but I've played enough tug of war with dogs to know it's just a trick. Right when I know she's about to yank my arm, I fling it away from her.

She wasn't supposed to let go. The coffeepot goes flying out of my hand, soars over the island like a wild, glitching robotic bird, and crashes into the fridge.

There's an explosion of glass. A siren of dogs. Coffee streaks down the stainless steel door of the fridge, all over the treehouse plans, and onto the floor.

Both parents come running.

"Sadie!" Mom screams. "What is going on?"

"Don't come in here! There's broken glass."

Mom stops at the edge of the crime scene. Dad gets a dustpan and broom.

"I was trying to get the coffeepot away from Sam," Sadie explains.

"What was he doing with it?"

"Pouring himself a second cup."

"*What?!* Since when are *you* drinking coffee?"

"I have a lot of things due tomorrow."

"You're eleven years old! You need sleep!"

"But Mom," I say, "if I get it all done by tomorrow, they won't take off points. If they don't take off points, I might be able to get As in three out of four classes. If I can get As in three out of four classes — and keep it up next semester — I might make honor roll. If I make honor roll five out of six semesters in middle school, they'll let me start taking AP classes right away in ninth grade. Miss Lopez told us that in high school you get *extra* GPA points for AP classes, which means I'll have a head start on other kids when I apply to college."

I look at Mom's face. It's perfectly still, except for the tears falling down her cheeks.

"I told you there should be no more homework in this home," Dad says cheerfully, sweeping up the glass.

That's when the phone rings.

"I'll get it," Sadie says. She tiptoes over to the telephone and answers. "Mr. Kalman," she says. "I'm glad you're up."

Sadie lights our way with the flashlight app on her cell phone. When we get to Mr. Kalman's front porch, I see the newspaper I picked up yesterday afternoon still sitting there.

The candle in the window, near the end of its wax, is flickering.

The door opens, and Mr. Kalman stands there wearing his fur slippers and plaid robe.

"Do you know what I caught Sam doing?" Sadie says.

"Poisoning the dogs, I hope."

"Drinking coffee. At three thirty in the morning."

"I could use a cup right now."

He turns and heads inside. We follow him in.

When we go past the candle, I ask him, "What's with the candle, Mr. Kalman?"

"It's for my wife, Miriam. Yesterday was her Yahrzeit."

"Is that like a birthday?"

"It's the opposite of a birthday, Sam. We light a candle on the anniversary of the person's death. A person we loved."

"Do you know *why* my eleven-year-old brother was drinking coffee at three thirty in the morning?"

Mr. Kalman shakes his head.

"Homework."

Mr. Kalman looks at the candle. He shakes his head again and says, "They're supposed to burn for twenty-four hours. I lit hers twenty-eight hours ago. She does that to me every year. Refuses to burn out."

"Maybe she's trying to tell you something," Sadie says.

"What, that I ought to go over there and blow out the candle?"

"That you ought to keep on burning too." She looks right at Mr. Kalman and says, "Don't we have one last appeal, to the US Supreme Court?"

"It's not so simple, Sadie. We've made our best arguments before two federal courts. Four justices shot us down."

"So you're giving up?"

Mr. Kalman looks away. "I told you I wouldn't be able to see it through."

"Mr. Kalman, if Oliver Brown in *Brown v. Board of Education* had given up, black and white students might still be going to segregated schools. If Miranda had given up, people could be arrested without being told their rights. If Jim Obergefell had given up, people couldn't marry the person they love. If we give up, nothing will change for this generation of kids. Nothing will change for Sam."

Mr. Kalman just stands there, looking at the candle.

"And Goliath wins," I say.

A saying pops out of Sadie's mouth. "You can't tear down a wall if you don't take a swing."

Mr. Kalman looks at her. "What's *that?*"

"One of Bernice's advice pills."

"Who's Bernice?"

"Our mom's parenting teacher," I explain. "She's always handing out little sayings."

"Tell me another."

"You can't prepare the path for the child, so prepare the child for the path."

He thinks about that one, tilts his head, then nods as if he agrees.

"Another."

"Failure is the greenhouse of success," Sadie says.

"Sleep or weep," I say.

"A consequence builds character."

"Follow through and you won't have to follow up."

Mr. Kalman looks at me. He looks at Sadie. He looks over at Mrs. Kalman's candle. Twenty-eight hours and still dancing.

"You can't tear down a wall if . . . ?"

"You don't take a swing," a voice says from across the room.

We all turn around and see Mom standing in the doorway.

She and Mr. Kalman exchange a long look. It's like they're having a whole conversation with just their eyes. Finally, he says, "Who wants to take a field trip?"

"Where to, Mr. Kalman?" I ask.

"Our nation's capital."

"We all do," Mom says.

Would you trade her to another team? I wouldn't.

18

ONE OF US FLIES
FIRST CLASS

Sunday afternoon, Sean and Sadie have just finished a marathon study session, and his Uber is out front. Sadie walks him onto the porch, which happens to be right next to the window of our front bathroom, where I *happen* to be through no fault of my own.

As Alistair says, it's the final step of a great meal.

The window is open. For ventilation purposes only.

"First we go to Washington," I hear Sadie say. "Then Mr. Kalman asks the court for a mandatory injunction against homework. At the same time he files our appeal of the Ninth Circuit Court's decision. Then we organize a huge march. We need you, Sean, every step of the way."

"I don't know, Sadie," Sean says. "We've got midterms coming up. You've got your Common App essay deadline. I mean, the Supreme Court—it's kind of a long shot."

I wait for my big sister, captain of the debate team and

winner of all those speaker points, to say something. But she's as mute as me in front of authority figures.

I wait some more. Not a single word from Sadie about fighting all the way, finishing the job, or keeping hope alive. No persuasive arguments along the lines of *we can't let all those kids down, can we?* Or, *I thought you were my boyfriend.* Or even, *Quitters never win and winners never quit.*

Maybe something's wrong with her, I think. Sore throat? Laryngitis?

So, very quietly, slowly, and respectfully, I stand up, lower the toilet seat, and climb onto it. Then I peek out the window.

The reason Sadie's not talking is that her mouth is busy.

When it's done being busy, know what Sean says?

"I'll go home and start packing."

I'm not sure if it would work on the members of the Supreme Court, but when it comes to your boyfriend or girlfriend, there's nothing more convincing than a kiss.

Monday morning, Alistair, Jaesang, Catalina, and I deliver notes from our parents to Miss Lochman.

"We're going to be absent next week," I say. "And while it's still legal, we feel obligated to do the homework. Our parents were wondering if you'd fax it to us at the hotel in DC?"

Actually, the deal we made is we can't go to DC unless

we promise to spend time on the flight home keeping up with our work.

"What's the name of the hotel?" Miss Lochman asks.

"The Watergate."

According to Mr. Kalman, the Watergate has a lot of history. A famous crime took place there. In 1972, the Democratic National Committee had their headquarters at the Watergate. Burglars broke into their offices, tapped phones, left transmitters under tables, and then got caught by a security guard.

Guess who they were working for.

Richard Nixon, the president of the United States! He wanted to know what the Democrats were planning to use against him in the election.

Nixon won. In "a landslide," Mr. Kalman told us. It took two years before the whole story came out. Congress wanted to throw Nixon out of office, but he resigned.

Ever since, whenever you hear the word *gate* at the end of another word, that means there's a scandal.

There's been Nannygate, Travelgate, Troopergate, Irangate, and a whole lot of other gates. I start to worry there's about to be a Homeworkgate.

"Are you sure it's a good idea to stay at that hotel?" I ask Mr. Kalman. "What if Livingston Gulch has friends there? They might tap our rooms and listen in on our strategy."

"We'll double-check the phones, Sam. If we find any bugs, we'll give them misinformation. Besides, the Watergate just came through a big renovation. The history's there and it's not there, if you know what I mean."

How can history be there and not there at the same time? Unless . . . paradox?

On Tuesday we wake up early, drop the dogs at a friend of my dad's, and head to the airport with Mr. Kalman. Not only are my parents getting a room of their own at the Watergate, they've got a row of their own on the plane. They're sitting in 17 while we're in 8 with Mr. Kalman. Right now Sadie is asking him for advice.

"Do you think I should go away to college?"

"It's a big world, Sadie. A young person should venture out into it."

"I probably won't even get in to the out-of-state schools."

"Why not? I thought that with your grades and the debate team . . ."

"My grades have gone down. I'll be lucky to hold on to a 3.5 GPA."

"Because of the case?"

She looks at me.

"I'm glad I did it, though. Win or lose, it feels right to try."

Sadie leans around Mr. Kalman and gives me a look that says, *Quit listening in.* I lean back against my seat and check out the in-flight entertainment.

The problem with sitting just three rows behind the first-class curtain is the smell of haute cuisine that hits our noses while we're nibbling on snack trays of cold bread, dry chicken breast, and wrinkly cherry tomatoes.

On the other side of the curtain, something good is being served. There's a creamy, cheesy, herby scent—I'm guessing fettuccine alfredo, but it's probably got company on the plate, some salmon or steak, too, with garlic butter. The smell is like a leash for Alistair, tugging his nose forward into the space between Mr. Kalman's seat and mine.

I can hear him sniffing.

Mr. Kalman can hear him sniffing too—and he doesn't even have his hearing aid in.

The call button in our row lights up, and soon a flight attendant comes down the aisle and asks Mr. Kalman, "May I help you, sir?"

"Is it possible to purchase an in-flight upgrade?"

"Would you like to move seats?"

"Are there any available in first class?"

"Well, yes. But we're already an hour into the flight."

"I wouldn't ask for a discount. You can charge me whatever you like."

The flight attendant looks at this eighty-five-year-old man surrounded by a bunch of kids.

"You want a quieter flight, don't you?"

Mr. Kalman smiles and hands him his credit card. The flight attendant reaches for it, but Mr. Kalman pulls it back.

"The food will be upgraded as well, won't it?"

"Yes, of course, sir."

He nods and hands him the card again.

Then Mr. Kalman turns around in his seat, which isn't so easy for a guy way past eighty who's probably never done yoga, and says, "Get up, Alistair. You're moving seats."

I hope Alistair makes a lot of money when he grows up. I can't imagine him ever flying coach again.

The newly renovated Watergate is an awesome hotel. Mr. Kalman upgrades our team to the Homework Suite. It's really called the Presidential Suite, but we've renamed it for luck. It has three huge rooms, a nice little kitchen (Alistair's happy), and a spectacular view of the Mall.

After we check in, we head out for a tour and Mr. Kalman's crash course on the Constitution. We already know the basics, how there are three branches of government—legislative, executive, and judicial.

The legislative, a.k.a. Congress, which is made up of the Senate and the House of Representatives, makes the laws.

The executive, a.k.a. the president, enforces the laws.

And the judicial, a.k.a. the Supreme Court and its subcourts, interprets the laws. They decide whether laws are "legal," or in the spirit of the Constitution. The whole system was designed to keep any one branch from getting too much power. Checks and balances, it's called.

The president is commander in chief of the military, but he has to ask Congress before he can declare war. Congress controls the money, so if they don't like what the president is doing, they can refuse to pay for it. Congress writes new laws, but they're called bills until the president signs them. If the president refuses to sign, that's a veto, and the bill dies.

If he signs and the people think the law is unfair, they can challenge it in federal court. If the Supreme Court says the law is unconstitutional, it gets canceled.

Mr. Kalman tells us the Supreme Court is the last guardian of the people's rights.

Say we're in a war and a student wants to protest it. He wears a black armband to school. A teacher asks him, *Why the black armband?* He says, *To show I'm against the war.* The next day the principal says, *Black armbands aren't allowed at school. If you don't take it off, we'll suspend you.*

Can they do that?

No, they can't. In 1969 the Supreme Court ruled that students "do not shed their constitutional rights . . . at the schoolhouse gate." (*Tinker v. Des Moines Independent School District.*)

Does that mean we can write whatever we want in the school newspaper?

No. Because in *Hazelwood School District v. Kuhlmeier* they ruled that the principal gets to edit the school paper.

And, at a school-supervised event, you can't hold up a

sign that encourages kids to take illegal drugs. (*Morse v. Frederick.*)

You can't make obscene campaign speeches, either. (*Bethel School District v. Fraser.*)

But you can pray in school, as long as you're private about it.

Can the school force you to pray? Nope. That would violate the Constitution's separation of church and state. (*Engel v. Vitale.*)

What if the football team wants to say a prayer before the game? Can they use the stadium's loudspeaker to lead it?

Not if it's a public school. (*Santa Fe Independent School District v. Doe.*)

Say you apply for a job at the mall. The store you want to work at has a dress code: "Classic East Coast collegiate style." But your own personal dress code calls for a hijab. Can the store turn you down?

No. In *Equal Employment Opportunity Commission v. Abercrombie & Fitch,* the Supreme Court ruled eight to one that an employer can't say no to an applicant based on her religious practices.

Can a state decide that blacks and whites (or any other racial or ethnic groups) can't eat at the same restaurants or go to the same schools? No way. Separate schools and drinking fountains are "inherently unequal." (*Brown v. Board of Education of Topeka, Kansas.*)

Can schools assign kids work to do beyond the school day? That's what we're here to find out.

"We've asked the court to issue a writ of certiorari," Mr. Kalman says. "It's a formal request to hear our appeal."

We're standing on the steps of the US Supreme Court, which looks like an ancient Greek monument with supertall columns holding it up. There are two sculptures, one of a woman holding a scale and the other of a man holding a tablet of laws.

"What do you mean, *request?*" Catalina says. "I told my whole church we were going all the way to the Supreme Court."

"The Supreme Court's not the school principal, Catalina. They get to pick which cases are heard. Most never are."

"You mean we might have come all this way for nothing?" Alistair says.

"What, you don't want to sightsee?"

"Maybe if we can try some restaurants. But I'd rather give the justices a piece of my mind."

"Well, then, we'd better get their attention."

He turns to Sadie and Sean and says, "Kids, it's time to twerk."

I don't think Mr. Kalman knows what twerking is. He means "tweet." But I've got to hand it to him. For a guy who only recently discovered the Internet, he's getting the hang of things pretty fast.

No. _____

In the
Supreme Court of the United States

SAMUEL E. WARREN,
Petitioner

v.

LOS ANGELES UNIFIED SCHOOL DISTRICT,
Respondent

**On Petition for Writ of Certiorari
to the United States Court of Appeals**

PETITION
FOR WRIT OF
CERTIORARI

AVI KALMAN
Filing as Prochain Ami

1180 Otsego Street
Valley Village, CA 91607
Telephone: (818) 990-1481
E-mail: akalman@gmail.com

Counsel for Petitioner

QUESTIONS PRESENTED

1) Does the policy of Respondent Los Angeles Unified School District of assigning additional tasks beyond the school day, a.k.a. "homework," violate the implied privacy rights of the Fourth Amendment to the United States Constitution?

2) Does that same policy also violate the Fourteenth Amendment's guarantee of Equal Protection Under the Law?

3) Is the pursuit of happiness by a minor a guaranteed right under the Constitution?

4) Under the Constitution of the United States, does a child have the right to a childhood, which cannot be denied without due process?

19

THE MARCH

Our **message goes out** in fewer than 140 characters: *Join the march against homework. 8 a.m. Friday. Lafayette park.*

Guess who lives across the street from that park. The president!

We boost our advertising with a new YouTube video, which we shoot at this jazz bar Mr. Kalman knows. I play Bob Marley's "Get Up, Stand Up" on the piano while Sean and Jaesang make up new lyrics: "Get up, stand up, it's in the Bill of Rights. / We got to gather, together. In peace to show our might. / So stand up, boot up, join the Homework Fight."

All across the country kids post a single word on their Instagrams: "March." Brothers and sisters work together on handmade NO HOMEWORK signs. Kids close to DC hop on bikes, boards, and blades. Their parents have no choice but to follow. On CNN we learn that a girl from Pennsylvania hijacked her school bus and they're on the way.

On Friday morning we come up from the subway station near Lafayette Square. I feel like we've just entered a football stadium packed with fans. Suddenly I'm hoisted up in the air like I'm the coach of the winning team. I look down and see I'm on Sean's shoulders. I look out and see an ocean of color—jackets, scarves, banners, and caps.

"Yowza!" Catalina says. "That's a lot of people."

Sadie hands me a bullhorn. "What's this for?"

"They're here for you, Sam. You have to lead the march."

Kid leader. I'm pretty sure that's an oxymoron.

My stomach flips. In my head, the Guided Meditation Lady reminds me to *breathe*.

Mr. Kalman reaches up and puts his hand on my arm. "It's always nice, Sam, to say thank you for coming."

The bullhorn is heavy in my hand and looks like the bottom half of a trumpet. I wish it *were* a trumpet. Then I'd know what to do.

"Sometime this century, Sam," Sadie says.

That's worse than an elbow. It works, though. It gets me to talk.

"Hello? I'm Sam Warren."

A wave of sound rises and almost knocks me down.

"Um," I say, and right away I feel stupid. What kind of leader leads with an *um?*

So I take a minute and think it through. What do I want to say? Why am I really here?

"I'm just one kid," I say, "who got fed up with what's happening to us all. We're not against school. We learn a lot in school. We've learned about people who changed things. But the textbooks don't say enough about the people who helped them. There is no way I would be here without all of you. So thank you for coming. And now we've got to let the Supreme Court know we're here. So come on, everybody, let's march!"

An even louder roar flies up from the crowd.

Sean sets me down and we start to walk. The Capitol police were worried about the size of our crowd, so they've routed the march along Pennsylvania Avenue toward the Peace Monument, then around the north side of the Capitol to the Supreme Court. Along the way, Catalina calls out names of important historic sites, while Alistair calls out names of restaurants. After a few blocks, I know where the FBI headquarters are, Fogo de Chão Brazilian Steakhouse, Ford's Theatre where Lincoln was shot, Central Michel Richard, the National Archives (home to the Declaration of Independence, the Constitution, and the Bill of Rights), and the Capital Grille, which Alistair heard has the best ribeye in town.

Soon I see four men in dark glasses and suits making their way toward me. My first thought: we just passed FBI headquarters and they've sent a few agents to arrest me for inciting a riot. But it turns out they're Secret Service agents guarding the president's son, who wanted to come over and say hi.

"I think what you're doing is awesome," he says. "But don't tell my dad."

"Thanks," I say. "I never saw you."

Then Alistair turns to a big, beefy Secret Service agent. He jerks toward the man but stops short. The agent leans back.

"Two for flinching!" Alistair says. And he punches the Secret Service guy twice on his right arm! Not hard, though. Alistair's crazy, but he doesn't have a death wish.

Jaesang just rolls his eyes, and we march on.

It's a little over two miles from the White House to the Supreme Court, but with so many people marching, no one gets tired. Along the route, lining both sides of Pennsylvania Avenue, crowds of people and their signs cheer us on:

MOMS AGAINST HOMEWORK.

SOS — SAVE OUR STUDENTS.

NO CHILDHOOD LEFT BEHIND.

One of the moms offers our mom a sign. She holds it up like she's the Statue of Liberty.

I'm worried about Mr. Kalman, though. The longest

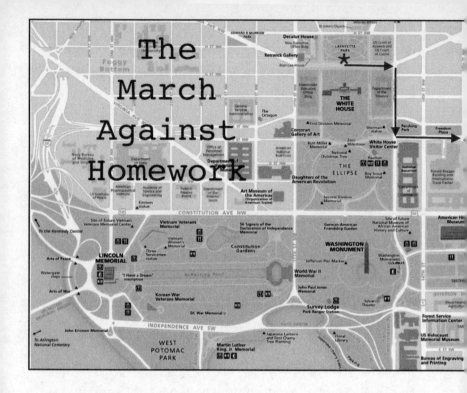

The March Against Homework

walk he's taken lately is from his mailbox to his front door. This much exercise might land him in the hospital, and then we'd never get to stand before the Supreme Court. I glance over at him, and to tell you the truth, I don't much like his color. A little gray. Not from the parka he's wearing, either. It's a gray from the inside.

"Mr. Kalman, how about sitting down for a minute?"

"I can make it, Sam. And if I keel over, think of the publicity we'll get. The justices will have to take our case."

"Yeah, but who's going to argue it?"

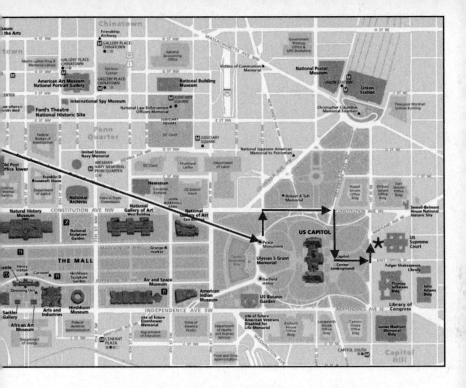

"Good point. I'd better stay on my feet."

Sadie and Sean each take one of Mr. Kalman's arms to steady him, and we march on.

We're almost at Columbus Circle when I hear a voice call out.

"Mr. Kalman! Mr. Kalman!"

We all turn and see a woman squeezing toward him through a wall of people. At first Mr. Kalman doesn't recognize her, but when she says her name, he sure does.

"Sul Jung Lee."

"Oh, my goodness! Sul Jung!"

She tries to get closer to him, but the wall of people is too thick. He calls to her over their heads.

"How are you? What became of you?"

"I'm the assistant band director at Stuyvesant High School in New York. We heard about the march. I wouldn't miss it for the world."

That's when I realize who she is. The girl whose case he argued before the Supreme Court. He reaches out to her, and their hands touch for just a second before the crowd pulls them apart.

"Hey, Mr. Kalman," she calls out.

He turns back.

"Second time's a charm!"

Then she raises a baton to a row of white-feathered hats behind her. She's brought her school's marching band to DC, and as the brass starts blowing, I swear Mr. Kalman is walking like he's twenty years younger.

We pick up Constitution Avenue, which takes us around the Capitol, and with all these historic buildings going by, it occurs to me that Mr. Powell and Miss Lopez should have brought the whole class on the march, because they'd learn a lot more history right here than they ever could from a textbook.

And guess what. The whole class *will* get to see. We just walked by a CNN news van. They're broadcasting live.

We come around to the east side of the Capitol, and I

recognize this place. It's where the helicopter takes off from when the old president leaves office after the new one's been sworn in. I wonder what that feels like, flying away from such a powerful job.

We cross First Street, and step onto the marble plaza of the Supreme Court.

Where ten Supreme Court police officers form a wall we can't cross.

"Hold it right there, Sam," Mr. Kalman says.

"We can't go onto the plaza?"

"I'm afraid not."

"What about the First Amendment?" I ask. "It says that 'Congress shall make no law . . . abridging the freedom of speech, or of the press; or the right of the people peaceably to assemble, and to petition the government for a redress of grievances.'"

"Yes, but in 2016 the Supreme Court let stand a lower court ruling in *Hodge v. Talkin* that said we have to stay on the sidewalk."

"That's crazy! How can the Supreme Court, which defends the rights of citizens to raise their voices in protest, say they can raise their voices everywhere but in front of the Supreme Court?"

"It's what you might call a paradox, Sam. And yet, it's the law."

"How will they hear us all the way from the sidewalk?"

"Oh, we'll make them hear."

And then, in his raspy old man's voice, Mr. Kalman shouts:

"*What do we want?*"

"*Free time!*"

"*When do we want it?*"

"*After four!*"

Mr. Kalman said it's up to the court whether or not they want to hear our case. With over a hundred thousand kids and their parents standing on their front sidewalk right now and spilling into the park across the street, do you really think they're going to turn us down? I mean, Chief Justice Reynolds has kids. And if the homework in his family is anything like the homework in ours, I'll bet they're texting him right now, begging him to take our case.

An hour goes by, then two. It's late in the afternoon when we get word from Sean, who's been streaming CNN on his smartphone, that Chief Justice Reynolds has called a special conference. Just before the sun sets, the bronze doors of the Supreme Court building open, and the clerk of the court steps out.

"Oyez, oyez, oyez!" he says into a megaphone. That's the Supreme Court's way of saying "listen, listen, listen." "The matter of *Warren v. Board of Education* will be heard."

The crowd behind me roars. Mr. Kalman doesn't miss a beat.

"Back to the hotel," he says. "We've got work to do."

20

THE HOMEWORK SUITE

Hello, room service? This is Alistair Martin in room — no, *suite* — 1209. We have a crew of hungry children up here and I'm wondering if you might send up a bowl — make that a platter — of spaghetti carbonara. Extra bacon, please, garlic bread on the side. Is your chef qualified to make those soft-shelled crab cakes I've seen on the cooking shows? Terrific. A triple order of those, too. Now, I hope you won't think I'm being picky, but my mother wants me to cut down on red meat. Any vegetarian options you recommend? A mushroom-quinoa burger on a gluten-free bun with a side of sweet potato fries and coleslaw? I'll give it a try. No, thank you, to the mayo. Yes, please, to the ketchup. In a little porcelain bowl if possible. I love those. Our own mini-bottle of ketchup, for keeps? That's even better. To drink . . . ? How about a hot chocolate, heavy on the marshmallows? And a Diet Coke *avec* caffeine. We've got a long night ahead. Oh, and you'd better throw in a side of broccoli or my mom'll kill me. But ask the chef to roast it if you don't mind—olive oil, garlic, and a handful of Parmesan cheese. I'm hoping he has a big hand. Dessert? *Hmmmmm.* We wouldn't say no to some *mousse au chocolat . . .* You're out of the mousse? I see. Crème brûlée *is* a good alternative, isn't it? Raspberries, this time of year? Flown in, huh? Okay. We'll try the crème brûlée with fresh raspberries, then. No, I think that's all. But hang on a sec."

Alistair covers the phone and turns to us. "You guys want anything?"

You might think it's easier to get work done in a hotel because there are fewer distractions. But the opposite is true. How many kids have an elevator at home with fourteen buttons to push? How many can go joy-riding in the halls on a luggage cart? There's a pool, a gym, and a rec room with a Ping-Pong table *and* foosball. Besides room service, you can eat at the twice-a-day buffet, with so many choices for your omelet that you could lose weight just walking up the line. Not to mention the people-watching in the lobby. I could spend a whole day making up stories behind all those faces.

And I might, too, if we weren't on a mission. But Mr. Kalman says we have work to do.

If a teacher assigns a report on a Supreme Court justice, chances are most kids will go on Wikipedia and copy and paste, maybe change a few words, and print in a super-big font so they meet the three-page requirement under the rubric. But the way Mr. Kalman assigns it, treating us like his partners instead of employees, makes us forget about the fourteen buttons in the elevator and the forty-seven omelet options; it blurs away the faces in the lobby and practically drains the hotel pool.

It makes us want to work for him. Because, really, we're working for ourselves.

"Everybody pick a justice," he says, dropping a stack of index cards on the wood table in his hotel suite. On each card is the name and face of a different Supreme Court justice.

Our hands plunge into the pile. We fight a little over the cards—Jaesang and I both reach for the same one; Sadie says she really wants Eleanor Cohen and Clement Williams, so we let her have them both (since she and Sean are older, they each have to pick two justices). Sean gets Justice DeFazio and Justice Fitzgerald. I let Jaesang take his pick between Rauch and Renfro, and he chooses Renfro. Catalina gets Justice Suerte. Alistair shouts, "I got the Chief! No way I'm trading." And Mr. Kalman smiles at the thin, wise face of Justice Rosenburg.

"This justice is for me," he says. Then he looks up at all of us. "I want you to find out everything you can about the justice in your hand. Childhood. Personality. Philosophy about the law. Anything that might give us an advantage when we walk into that courtroom."

"Shouldn't we be focusing on the law?" Jaesang asks.

"It's not just a legal argument we're trying to win," Mr. Kalman explains, "but the hearts and minds of nine human beings. Maybe you'll discover something in their biographies that will make them sympathetic to the cause. Remember, Supreme Court justices were once kids just like you."

He steps to a whiteboard he had sent up from a conference room. He draws three columns on it.

"As soon as you've done your research, we'll divide the justices into three categories."

He labels each column: "On Our Side," "Not Sure," and "Heaven Help Us."

"Any questions?"

Alistair has one. "Can we work in partners?"

"Sure, why not?"

That's another difference between homework and hotel work. Here you're part of a team.

So we get to work. Sean uses his cell phone as a mobile hot spot because he doesn't trust the hotel's Wi-Fi. After all, this is the Watergate. We have enough iPads, laptops, and smartphones to do our "preliminary round of research." Later, if we need it, there's the law library at Georgetown University. Mr. Kalman can get us in.

I look down at the face on my card. Justice Gaylor S. Rauch. Justice Rauch, "Gorch" to his friends, is the newest justice on the Supreme Court. He seems like a pretty strait-laced guy. He grew up in Colorado and went to Catholic school and has two school-age daughters. Both his parents were lawyers, and his mom was the first woman to head the Environmental Protection Agency.

As a boy, Justice Rauch studied a lot, but he also liked to play outside. According to him, "There are few places closer to God than walking in the wilderness or wading in a trout stream."

Sounds like he'd be pretty receptive to a kid who *wishes* he could walk in the wilderness or wade in a trout stream but has to do homework all day.

On the other hand, Justice Rauch got straight As all the way to Harvard Law School. Plus he went to Oxford for a philosophy degree. What's he going to say to a boy who got suspended?

Since he's brand-new on the court, I have to dig into some of Rauch's decisions on the Tenth Circuit Court of Appeals. That's where I find out something that really warms my heart.

Justice Rauch believes in a kid's right to burp!

This seventh-grader in New Mexico wanted to crack up the kids in gym class, so he started fake-burping really loud. The teacher told him to stop. He kept on burping. She sent him into the hall with the door open. He kept on burping. The burps got louder and louder and funnier and funnier. The coach got angrier and angrier. When she couldn't take it anymore, she called the resource officer, a.k.a. campus cop.

In New Mexico it's a criminal offense to disrupt a school

activity. Most people take "school activity" to mean an assembly, a graduation, or a college president's workday. But this school took it to mean any school activity, even a boring PE class. They could have given the burping kid detention or even suspended him for a few days. But they wanted to make a point. So the resource officer handcuffed the kid and drove him to Juvy. His mom sued, claiming the punishment was way too harsh. She lost, appealed, and lost again in the Tenth Circuit.

Justice Rauch wrote a dissent, siding with the kid and his mom.

Sometimes the law can be an ass, he wrote, quoting Charles Dickens. *If a seventh-grader starts trading fake burps for laughs in gym class, what's a teacher to do? Order extra laps? Detention? A trip to the principal's office? Maybe. But then again, maybe that's too old school. Maybe today you call a police officer. And maybe today the officer decides that, instead of just escorting the now compliant thirteen-year-old to the principal's office, arresting him would be a better idea. So out come the handcuffs and off goes the child to juvenile detention. My colleagues suggest the law permits exactly this option. Respectfully, I remain unpersuaded.*

Bottom line: He sided with the kid. Maybe he'll be on our side, too.

We go on with our research. Alistair's room service feast comes and goes. And the hotel suite gets quieter than a classroom during the CAASPP test. Only instead of the scratch of number 2 pencils and the creak of erasers on answer sheets, you hear keyboards clicking and papers shuffling. It's so quiet I can hear Mr. Kalman take a sip of coffee.

I look over and see Sadie reading a *New York Times* article on her iPad. The headline says, "No Argument: Williams Keeps Seven-Year Silence."

Sean is reading something called "The Boundaries of Privacy" by Daniel DeFazio, and Catalina is looking at a Google Earth image of some buildings near Yankee Stadium. Mr. Kalman flips through an illustrated biography of RBR, Rachel Braun Rosenburg. Alistair and Jaesang are studying the Constitution.

Meanwhile Mom and Dad are doing something *their* parents did back in the 1960s — demonstrating. Mom FaceTimes Sadie from the sidewalk outside the Supreme Court.

"What do we want?" Mom shouts.

"Family time!" the others shout back.

"When do we want it?"

"After four!"

That's one argument that really convinced Mom. Kids spend so much time on homework, they don't sit down and eat with their families anymore.

But down the block, there's another point of view. Teachers are chanting, "Supreme Court justices, watch your reach. Students gotta practice what teachers teach!"

And this from another group of teachers: "Hey, hey, ho, ho, this laziness has got to go!"

If we're so lazy, how'd we make it all the way to the Supreme Court?

We've been working for so long that Alistair gets hungry again. He and I ask Mr. Kalman if we can take a break and go down to the hotel gift shop for snacks.

Mr. Kalman says sure. "And bring me back some Juicy Fruit gum, will you? You can put it on the room."

Alistair gives me a look that says, *I wonder what else we can put on the room.*

I have to say there's a pretty awesome gift shop at the newly reopened Watergate Hotel. Besides the usual racks of candy, gum, souvenirs, and games, there's a whole section of guidebooks to Washington, DC, and other books on Congress, the presidency, and the Supreme Court. While Alistair is busy cuddling a stuffed panda, I browse the shelves to see if there's anything on my man, Justice Gaylor S. Rauch.

A different kind of book catches my eye. A small paperback with a plain cover and the words "Supreme Court Rules" on the front.

"Sam, check this out. He speaks Chinese."

Alistair pulls the string on the stuffed panda, and sure enough there's a squeaky voice saying something like, "I'm on a ten-year loan to America. Come see me before I get shipped home," but I can't be sure of the translation because, no kidding, it's really in Chinese.

Not the *Supreme Court Rules*, though. It would have seemed like Chinese to me just three months ago, but now it's in English I can understand. It tells all the rules and procedures for arguing a case before the court. I figure we'd better buy this and give it to Mr. Kalman because it's been more than thirty years since he faced "the bench," as it's known around here.

"Come on," I say to Alistair after I grab a few packs of Juicy Fruit for Mr. Kalman and a dozen Crunch bars for the team.

But Alistair hesitates. It's like love at first sight with the stuffed panda.

"Seriously? You're getting the panda?"

"I can't help it. It's so cute."

He holds it up to me and makes its left paw wave.

"Alistair . . ."

"I won't charge it to the room. My mom gave me a twenty for just this sort of thing."

"Wouldn't you rather put the twenty toward a zoo ticket? Then you could see the real panda."

"What if it's not there on the day we go? They get sick sometimes. Or they're inside sleeping."

"You can always come back for the stuffed one."

"It might be sold."

He's having a hard time with this decision. And I'm having a hard time waiting for him to decide.

Finally he nods, but instead of putting the stuffed panda back where it was, he tucks it behind a fishing magazine. As an afterthought, he grabs a biography of Chief Justice Reynolds.

We show our room key to the lady behind the cash register.

"I still need a signature," she says.

"Get it from him," Alistair says. "It'll be worth more."

21

HEAVEN HELP US

After lunch on Sunday — this time Catalina and Jaesang did the ordering, pizza all around — Mr. Kalman rolls the top sheet of his legal pad over and says, "Let's start with the Chief."

Alistair takes his last bite of pizza crust and a swig of Coke, then stands to face us all. He rolls up his sleeves — both arms are tattooed with notes — and starts to talk.

"John Reynolds. Captain of his high school football team and regional champ in wrestling. His first major case: *Hedgepeth v. Washington Metropolitan Transit Authority*. I can hardly pronounce that. The city of Washington, DC, had a rule in the subways. No food allowed. I mean, none. If you were caught eating in the station or on the train, you'd get a *big fine*. Now, there was this twelve-year-old girl on her way home after school. She was hungry. I can relate to that. On her way to the station, she stopped at a McDonald's and bought some french fries. The train was due any minute, so it's not like she had time to eat. But while her friend went to buy the tickets, the smell of the french fries coming from her backpack made her hungrier . . . and hungrier . . . until she couldn't take it anymore. She reached in . . . pulled out a single french fry and tossed it into her mouth.

"The transit cops swooped in and arrested her, handcuffs and all, then dragged her down to Juvy. They held her there for three hours until her mom came to pick her up. The family sued. If the girl had been a grownup, they argued, she would have gotten off easy, with just a citation. But because she was a kid, they put her through hell. For one french fry."

Alistair waits for this to sink in. We've all got terrified looks on our faces.

"Guess who Reynolds sided with."

"The girl," Sean says. "It's an equal protection and due process violation."

"The cops."

We sit there in stunned silence as Alistair steps over to the whiteboard and writes "Reynolds" under "Heaven Help Us."

Next Sadie clicks her laptop, and Clement Williams appears.

"Clement Williams. Born in 1948 in St. Simons Island, Georgia. Appointed by Bush One in '91. He's been on the bench for twenty-six years, and he never talks."

"What do you mean he never talks?" I say.

"Never talks during oral arguments. Never asks questions or makes comments. He just sits there. Stone silent."

"Why?"

"It has to do with Justice Williams's childhood, Sam. His ancestors were slaves, and he spent his early childhood in a remote part of Georgia where people still spoke an African-English dialect called Gullah. Later, as the only black student in an all-white school, Williams took a lot of teasing for the way he talked. So he developed what he calls the habit of listening instead."

"Maybe he'll listen to us, then," Catalina says.

"Well, Catalina, here's what Williams wrote in a 2007 case about freedom of speech. And I quote: 'The Constitution does not afford students the right to free speech in public schools.'"

"In other words—" I say.

"Heaven help us," we all say.

Sadie tapes Williams next to Reynolds.

When it's Sean's turn, he presents Justice Fitzgerald. "Leading proponent of using foreign or international law as an aid to interpreting the US Constitution."

"Translation, Sadie?"

"He's willing to consider what the courts in other countries have said about an issue. So if we can find a foreign ruling about homework, it might help our case."

"Also, Justice Fitzgerald is generally thought of as a swing vote, meaning he can go either way."

"Just don't call him that to his face," Mr. Kalman adds. "He hates being called the swing vote."

We decide to put Fitzgerald in the "Not Sure" column.

Sean also picked Justice DeFazio. "A libertarian," he says.

"There's a librarian on the Supreme Court?"

"No, Alistair, that word is *li-ber-TAR-ian*. It's someone who wants to keep the government out of our private lives."

"In other words—"

"On our side!"

I can see why Sadie fought for Eleanor Cohen. "Cohen's the youngest of the Supreme Court justices. First woman dean of Harvard Law School and something of a rebel. When she was thirteen she demanded equal time for bar and bat mitzvahs—equality for boys and girls—and she got the rabbi to compromise. So it seems she'd favor a nation of children fighting for their rights. But—"

Alistair and I exchange a look. "There's always a but."

"Here it comes," Sadie continues. "Her mom was a teacher who once made a fifth-grade girl cry."

"Because she didn't do her homework?" Catalina asks.

"Because she didn't try her best."

We all stop to think about that. If I didn't try my best on something, and a teacher called me out for that, I'd think she was a good teacher. But if she made me feel bad after I did try my best, I'd think she was a monster.

Mr. Kalman asks Sadie where she'd put Justice Cohen.

"Have to go with 'Not Sure' on this one."

All eyes turn to Jaesang, who holds up Stuart Renfro.

"Not much to say about this guy," Jaesang says. "His father was a lawyer for—guess who."

We all shrug.

"The San Francisco Board of Education."

"Heaven help us!"

Jaesang writes him next to Reynolds and Williams.

When Catalina speaks, it's like the topic is "My Hero." "Cecilia Suerte grew up in a tenement neighborhood near Yankee Stadium. She's a big Yankees fan. Her parents were Puerto Rican and spoke only Spanish at home. When Cecilia was nine, her *papi* died of heart disease. Her *mami* had to raise Cecilia and her brother, Juan, alone. She bought them an Encyclopedia Britannica and made them read one page every night. Cecilia's favorite book series was Nancy Drew. Her favorite TV show was *Perry Mason*. She was on the debate team, like you guys, and grew up to be, well, you know. Oh, and Juan, he grew up to be a doctor."

Mr. Kalman looks at us, and Sadie says, "Nancy Drew? *Perry Mason*? The Yankees?"

"On our side," we all say.

Catalina smiles and adds Suerte's name to "On Our Side." But Mr. Kalman erases "Suerte" and writes her in the middle, under "Not Sure."

"What are you doing?" Sadie asks.

"Overriding you. That encyclopedia on the shelf might come back to bite us."

Then Catalina gets up. "Just because we don't want homework doesn't mean we don't want to learn," she says.

And she puts Justice Suerte back under "On Our Side."

Next up: Gaylor S. Rauch.

"The newest justice on the court," I tell them. "Thinks there's no place closer to God than a trout stream. Loves to spend time with his kids in nature. And in 2016, he upheld a kid's right to burp in class."

"Sam," Catalina says, "think about which president picked him. Put him under 'Heaven Help Us'!"

"He's for freedom of speech," Sean says, adding a burp for emphasis. "Put him 'On Our Side'!"

"Sam, he's your justice," Mr. Kalman says. "What do you think?"

I have to go with my gut on this one. On one side is the trout stream and the burping boy. Those give me a warm, fuzzy feeling. On the other is the fact that he's brand-new on the court, so we don't really know what he's thinking.

Altogether it adds up to . . .

"Not Sure."

"My justice, Rachel B. Rosenburg, was one of nine

women in her law school class. The dean said that women shouldn't be there because they were taking spots that men should have. But Rachel B. Rosenburg persevered and graduated first in her class. She's the oldest member of the court but still works out every day in the gym—which is more than I can say for myself—and she's never missed a case. She fights hard for the rights of women and children. She adored her husband and was devastated when he died. But she went back to work, because her other love has always been the law."

Mr. Kalman uncaps a dry erase marker. The only sound in the room is the squeaky noise it makes as he writes "Rachel Braun Rosenburg" under "On Our Side."

Nine justices. Three "On Our Side," three "Not Sure," three "Heaven Help Us." We knew it was going to be a long shot.

Mr. Kalman, who took notes on everything we said, hands his legal pad to Sadie and tells her, "Type these up or me."

Sadie looks stunned. Every page on the legal pad is full. "What am I, your secretary?"

"Consider it community service. It'll look good on your college applications."

That night when we're all in pajamas and ready for bed,

Alistair asks Mr. Kalman for a story about what it was like when he was a kid. Jaesang, Catalina, and I want to hear too, so we all gather around him and listen.

"As childhoods go, Alistair," Mr. Kalman says, "mine was delightfully dangerous."

"How so?"

"There were no adults around."

"You were an orphan, Mr. Kalman?" I ask.

"Just an independent kid, Sam. My parents owned a deli in the Bronx and were working all the time. I was more or less left alone."

"How did you get to see your friends?"

"By walking out the back door and into the alley. There, I'd meet up with my pals. We'd head off to wage daily battle, almost to the death."

"You were in a gang?"

"More like a team. We played stickball. The Jewish kids against the Italians or the Irish. And what we couldn't settle with sticks, we'd settle with fists."

"Fights, huh?" Alistair says, eyes widening with interest. Sadie and Sean come in from the other room to listen.

"Fact of the matter is, I was a scrawny kid. The only thing I had going for me was my mouth. Sometimes, fighting words spewed forth."

"Did you ever win a fight?"

"Never won. Never lost."

Never won, never lost. Delightfully dangerous. My head is spinning with paradoxes.

"How can you never win *and* never lose at the same time?" Jaesang asks.

"Let me tell you about the mighty Joe Mancuso. He was big, strong, and bearded, while the rest of us only dreamed of shadows on our upper lips. One time we got into an epic fight. I forget what started it, probably something I said, but the rules were if you wanted the fight to be over, you had to say uncle. Joe had me pinned to the ground with his big knees on my chest and my blood on his fist. 'Say uncle,' he barked. 'Say it or I'll hit you again.' I shook my head. He hit me again. 'Say uncle *now*,' he said, along with some other words you don't need to hear. I shook my head. He hit me again. This went on for, oh, half an hour at least. Bands of boys from the neighborhood, Jewish boys, Italians, Irish, all the kids whose parents were hard at work, gathered around us to see if Kalman would break down and say the word. But I never did. Finally, Joe began to tremble. He climbed off me and sat there in the alley, and in front of all those other boys, he wept.

"Imagine big, bearded Joe, king of the alley, laid flat by his own heaving sobs.

"I got up, wiped the blood from my mouth, and crawled over to him.

"'Why, Joe?' I said, putting my hand on his shoulder. 'Why the hell are you crying?'

"'Because you won't say uncle,' he said. 'And if you won't say uncle, how can I ever win?'

"I haven't thought about Joe Mancuso in a long time. But somebody," he says, looking over at Sadie, "made me think of him the other day."

Mr. Kalman puts out the light, and we all head off to bed. I don't need the Guided Meditation Lady to help me fall asleep. I just think about the scrawny little boy who wouldn't say uncle.

Tomorrow, I hope, neither will we.

22

WARREN V. BOARD OF EDUCATION

Sadie is the first one up. She walks past Jaesang, Alistair, and me in the sitting room and opens the door to Mr. Kalman's room, where he's still asleep in the king-size bed.

She's already dressed in her fancy Supreme Court clothes. She holds a large envelope in her hand.

Through the open door I hear her say, "I typed up your notes."

Mr. Kalman sits up and blinks away sleep.

"I'm worried about Justice Cohen," Sadie starts in. "Both her brothers are teachers. On CNN this morning they showed a big crowd of teachers against us."

"Is there coffee?" Mr. Kalman asks.

I get up and brew a pot in the suite's mini-kitchen. As soon as it's ready, I take a cup to Mr. Kalman, who's busy picking out clothes for his return appearance at the

Supreme Court. I see him hesitate between a blue tie and an orange one.

I hand him his coffee and point to the orange one.

"I think you'll be able to swing Justice Fitzgerald," Sadie says. "Sean found out that the Supreme Court of Canada gave one family the right to refuse homework."

Mr. Kalman sips the coffee, nods, and smiles at me as if to say, *Nicely brewed, Sam.*

Then he opens a small box on the table and pulls out a pair of silver cufflinks, which he introduces as "my lucky pair."

"Did you wear them last time?" I ask.

"No, those I gave away."

Mr. Kalman heads toward the bathroom. Sadie follows him, still talking. "And Sam was reading the Bill of Rights yesterday. He wanted to know what counts as *excessive fines*. As in, *excessive fines shall not be imposed*? And I said they mean money, and he said—tell him what you said, Sam."

"It could also mean time, couldn't it? Because with all the time we spend on homework, it feels like an excessive fine."

"Think you could use that?"

Mr. Kalman stops and turns around. "Sadie," he says, "I appreciate the help, but at the moment you're infringing on one of my Fourth Amendment rights."

"Which one?" she asks.

"Privacy."

And he shuts the bathroom door.

· · ·

Downstairs in the buffet line, there's a traffic jam of trays. Alistair is waiting for his fourth waffle, and Catalina, a strict vegetarian, is making the omelet chef swear on his entire line of maternal ancestors that no ham touched the pan. Eventually the rest of us catch up, but with so many choices — bagels, bear claws, French toast, bacon, cereal, and those omelets with the infinite add-ins — I'm just not that hungry. Neither is Sadie. There's a single croissant on her tray. I think we're both too nervous to eat.

Mom has saved a big table, and just as we're sitting down to it, Mr. Kalman steps into the dining room looking very convincing, I've got to say, in a blue suit and orange tie.

"Mr. Kalman," Mom says, "you look like you're on your way to court."

"That's exactly where I'm headed. There's a briefing with the clerk in twenty minutes."

Sadie shoves a bite of croissant into her mouth, takes a quick sip of juice, and springs up. Mr. Kalman looks at Sadie and seems sorry to have to tell her, "For attorneys only. You have to be a member of the Supreme Court Bar to come to the briefing."

I guess he remembers the rules, after all.

"I'll see you all up there, though. Ten o'clock sharp."

Sadie sighs and sinks back down. But then Mr. Kalman

calls her over. He pulls her off to the side, and I lean back in my chair.

Not snooping, just stretching.

"I'm sorry I didn't have time to shop," he says.

He tucks some folded-up money into her jacket pocket.

"Mr. Kalman," she says, "what for?"

"Today's your birthday, isn't it? December eleventh?"

Oh no. We totally forgot Sadie's birthday!

"Who told you?"

"Sean did. He came to wish me luck this morning. Said the day was bound to be lucky because it's the day you were born."

Sadie smiles. "But you didn't have to get me anything."

"It's not every day a girl turns eighteen."

Win or lose today, I think to myself, we'd better take her out to celebrate.

Mr. Kalman starts to head off, but Sadie calls after him.

"Mr. Kalman, wait!"

He turns back.

"What's it like? Arguing in front of the Supreme Court?"

He thinks about it for a second. "Ever play baseball, Sadie?"

"I did two years of Little League when I was younger."

"Well, imagine standing at home plate, only you're not facing one pitcher, but nine of them, from all sides. Instead of baseballs, they're throwing questions that you probably haven't thought about, and just as you start to answer one, another one comes from the right. You turn to answer that and a new one flies in from the left, and then from the center, two more. You're at bat for only thirty minutes, but the questions keep sailing in from every side, and you can't let a single one go by because the justices of the Supreme Court, well, they only throw strikes."

"Wow. You must be nervous."

"I am a little. But as long as I start out with the right words, everything will be fine. 'Mr. Chief Justice, and may it please the court . . .' That's how you always begin. Once those words are spoken, the rest will follow."

He turns and walks away.

"Good luck today," she calls after him. "We'll be there watching."

He puts up his hand to wave but doesn't look back.

After breakfast we all go up to change. My dad helps Jaesang with his tie, and Mom helps Catalina brush her hair — she wants to wear it down today like Justice Suerte wore hers in an old yearbook picture Catalina found. Alistair is looking mighty slick, I have to say, in his Hollywood Suit Outlet suit and thin black tie. His hair is all spiky because he borrowed too much gel from Sean, so while we're in the elevator I swipe some off his head and give my hair a lift too.

When we step out of the hotel, we find Sadie pacing back and forth like it's 9:55 instead of 9:25.

"Come on," she says, "we don't want to be late."

Dad motions to a cab driver at the front of a line, but the hotel doorman gives us some advice. "If you're heading up to the Supreme Court today, you're better off on the metro.

Your homework case is drawing a huge crowd." He tells us to take the Orange Line from Foggy Bottom to Capitol South. We'll be there in thirteen minutes.

We speed walk to the metro station and head downstairs to the trains. As we're passing through the turnstile, I see a pair of transit cops walking their beat. Alistair sees them too. He throws up his empty hands and shouts:

"No french fries!"

A breeze from the tracks lifts Catalina's hair. Soon we're on our train.

When we showed up in Lafayette Park for the march, there were a lot of people, and it brought a flock of humming-birds to my stomach. But this crowd, the one in front of the Supreme Court, makes that crowd look like Playmobil people and those birds feel like origami cranes. What I see in front of me now are two armies facing each other from behind barricades, and what I feel is a murder (perfect word, by the way) of crows pecking my guts out.

A kid holding up one end of a NO HOMEWORK banner recognizes me from YouTube.

"Hey, there he is! There's Sam Warren!"

A boys' soccer team calls out, "Give 'em hell, Sam!" and a whole Girl Scout troop screams, "We love you, Sam!"

What's a boy to do but blush and wave? And then I see a familiar face in the crowd. A face I can hardly believe is here because it's so far from home.

"Mr. Trotter? What are you doing here?"

"Pulling for you, Sam. Imagine what the school orchestra could do if the kids had more practice time."

I reach across the line of Washington, DC, police officers, and I fist bump my music teacher.

In case you've never been inside the US Supreme Court —and not a lot of people have—let me try to tell you what it's like. You know how when you visit a cathedral, a concert hall, or a really old forest, no grownup has to tell you to settle down? The place itself lets you know that it would appreciate a little silence. And you naturally respect that. Maybe, because so much has already gone on there before you showed up, you just want to be still. You want to take it all in.

That's the feeling I get when we walk into the Supreme Court. All the noise from the demonstrators outside gets swallowed up by the bronze doors, and we hear the clink of coins and keys and the thud of cell phones being dropped into security trays as we pass through the metal detectors; then there's the squeak of shoes on the polished marble floor and the hushed conversation. But even those sounds fade away as we go from the lobby into the courtroom itself, where I get that cathedral feeling, and for some reason it makes me feel small.

But also big with the possibility that we'll win.

Small and big at the same time.

Maybe the justices were right to keep things quiet on the plaza. From the marble steps to the bronze doors and beyond, there's something sacred about this place.

I look up and see twin American flags, one in the left corner and one in the right, and I think of the two statues seated outside, *Contemplation of Justice* and *Authority of Law*. Between the flags are four marble columns with a red velvet curtain behind them. And in front of the curtain is a long raised table with nine empty chairs.

The bench.

Facing that long table are two smaller ones for the two opposing teams: the *appellants* (us) and the *appellees* (them).

There's a lectern between the tables, where Mr. Kalman is going to stand when it's his turn. From there he'll look up at a hanging clock. According to the Supreme Court rules, you have thirty minutes to make your arguments. The justices can interrupt you as often as they want, but when those thirty minutes are done, so are you.

That's more pressure than penalty kicks in soccer, or the last thirty minutes of a standardized test.

And guess who's already seated at the appellees' table, looking calm and confident in his green suit.

Livingston Gulch.

Mr. Kalman hasn't come in yet, though. He's probably still with the clerk, going over procedures.

We all find seats together in the visitors' section — Mom, Dad, Sadie, Sean, Jaesang, Alistair, Catalina, and me.

I look up at the official clock: 9:55. I look over at Sadie, who mouths, "Where's Mr. Kalman?" I shrug because I don't know.

When the clock turns to 9:59, I start to worry.

"He should be here by now," I say, and just then we hear the marshal of the court pound his gavel.

"The Honorable Chief Justice, and the Associate Justices of the Supreme Court of the United States," he announces.

It's not like in the lower courts, where you spend forever waiting around. The Supreme Court starts on time. And it's not like the lower courts, where someone has to say, "All rise." All *automatically* rise as the red velvet curtain parts in two places. From the opening on the left, four justices step out wearing fancy robes: Justice Fitzgerald, Justice Williams, Justice Rosenburg, and Justice Renfro.

Then the next four — the junior ones — step out from the right: Justice DeFazio, Justice Suerte, Justice Cohen, and my guy, Justice Rauch.

Finally, from the center, Chief Justice Reynolds appears. Alistair can't contain himself. "That's the Chief! I picked him!"

As soon as the Chief sits, the marshal of the court says, "Oyez, oyez, oyez! All persons having business before the Honorable, the Supreme Court of the United States, are admonished to draw near and give their attention, for the court is now sitting. God save the United States and this Honorable Court!"

How about God save my lawyer? Where in DC is he?

I look desperately at Mom and Dad, but they just shake their heads.

What happens in the next sixty minutes is so crazy-fast that if I write it down, you're not going to believe that a boy who scores in the 80th percentile on his standardized tests could remember it all word for word. So I'm about to do what teachers tell us never to do. I'm going to copy and paste.

Remember that app I mentioned, PocketJustice? The one that has transcripts and recordings of actual Supreme Court cases? Well, here's the transcript from mine. And if you don't believe me, get the app yourself. It's free on Google Play and the Apple store. You can listen along as you read. (The stuff in parentheses isn't part of the transcript. It's just me making things clear.)

TRANSCRIPT

ORAL ARGUMENT ON BEHALF OF THE PETITIONERS

CHIEF JUSTICE REYNOLDS: Thank you, Marshal. We'll hear arguments this morning in Case 12-09121, *Warren v. Board of Education*. Mr. Avi Kalman filing as *prochain ami* to Samuel E. Warren, a minor.

Mr. Kalman, you may begin . . .

Mr. Kalman?

Is Mr. Kalman in the courtroom?

Was he at your briefing this morning, Clerk?

CLERK OF THE COURT: Yes, he was, Mr. Chief Justice.

CHIEF JUSTICE REYNOLDS: Did he mention that he would be late to arguments?

CLERK OF THE COURT: No, sir, he did not.

CHIEF JUSTICE REYNOLDS: Well, we can't proceed without the named attorney. Is the appellant here? Mr. Sam Warren?

SAM WARREN: Um, that's me, sir.

CHIEF JUSTICE REYNOLDS: Are *you* prepared to begin arguments in this case?

(Everyone laughs, which doesn't make me feel very good.)

SAM WARREN: No. But my sister is.

(At this point Sadie shrivels up, practically on the floor. Sean and Catalina have to lift her to standing.)

CHIEF JUSTICE REYNOLDS: Miss Warren?

SADIE WARREN: I, uh, Mr. Chief Justice, if you'll just give our counsel a little more time—

JUSTICE RAUCH: Would you like us to sit here while he waits for an Uber?

(More laughter from the crowd.)

SADIE WARREN: No, I . . . I mean, he should be here any minute. He has to be here.

JUSTICE RENFRO: The sensible thing to do in a situation like this is to postpone the case. We'll hear it in six months.

UNIDENTIFIED BOY FROM VISITORS' SECTION: Six months? The school year'll be over by then. And the homework in seventh grade is even worse!

(That's Alistair, as I'm sure you can guess.)

JUSTICE ROSENBURG: Why *not* let the young lady make the arguments?

(Sadie's head starts rocking side to side like crazy.)

LIVINGSTON GULCH: Because, Justice Rosenburg, that would be a violation of the Supreme Court rules.

(Gulch has his own copy. Of course. He reads aloud from it.)

"Only lawyers who have been admitted to the Bar of the Supreme Court may argue before it."

(But guess what! I have my own copy too! I jump up and read.)

SAM WARREN: "An attorney not admitted to the Bar of this Court but otherwise eligible for admission under Rule 5.1 may be permitted to argue *pro hac vice* [pro hawk vee'chay]. 'For this occasion only.'"

LIVINGSTON GULCH: Rule 5.1 — "To qualify for admission to the Bar of this Court, an applicant must have been admitted to practice in the highest court of a State, Commonwealth, Territory or Possession . . . for a period of at least three years."

SAM WARREN: She *has* practiced law in the highest court of a state. She's been doing mock trial since ninth grade. And that takes place in a federal courthouse.

LIVINGSTON GULCH: "Must not have been the subject of any adverse disciplinary action pronounced or in effect during that three-year period—"

SAM WARREN: She's never been suspended. I have, but—

LIVINGSTON GULCH: "And must appear to the Court to be of good moral and professional character."

(Okay, so Sadie has purple hair. But she's dressed really nicely. And the justices shrug like they're fine with the way she looks.)

LIVINGSTON GULCH: "Applicant must also have attained the legal age of adulthood in the state where he or she resides." That's California. She's got to be eighteen.

SAM WARREN: She *is* eighteen. Today's her birthday.

LIVINGSTON GULCH: We'd need proof of some kind. A birth certificate. The long form.

UNIDENTIFIED MAN FROM VISITORS' SECTION: I'm her father. And I'm telling you it's her birthday. My girl is eighteen today.

LIVINGSTON GULCH: I'd have to hear it from the lady who gave birth to her.

CHIEF JUSTICE REYNOLDS: We'll accept a sworn affidavit from her mom.

(This is a problem. Sadie looks at Mom, who stands up.)

UNIDENTIFIED WOMAN FROM VISITORS' SECTION: Mr. Chief Justice, her mother is no longer living. But as her stepmom since the girl was six, I can assure you that Sadie Warren is of excellent moral character and a blessing to her family. She stands up for what's right. She's true to herself. She's an inspiration to me.

CHIEF JUSTICE REYNOLDS: And that's your unbiased opinion?

UNIDENTIFIED WOMAN FROM VISITORS' SECTION: Yes, it is.

(Sadie turns all the way around and looks at Mom. They keep looking at each other until the Chief chimes in.)

CHIEF JUSTICE REYNOLDS: All right, then, let's admit her to the Bar and get the proceedings underway.

LIVINGSTON GULCH: What about the fee?

CHIEF JUSTICE REYNOLDS: What fee?

LIVINGSTON GULCH: "The fee for admission to the Bar and a certificate bearing the seal of the Court is $200, payable to the United States Supreme Court." Rule 5.5.

(At this point Dad reaches into his wallet, but he doesn't have that much cash on him. Alistair pulls out his twenty, and Jaesang comes up with another twenty, and other people start pitching in, but then I see Sadie reaching into her pocket and unfolding two crisp hundred-dollar bills. Her face is all flushed like she's trying to figure something out.)

SADIE WARREN: Do you take cash?

(She hands the clerk two hundred-dollar bills—the birthday money Mr. Kalman gave her. Then she walks up to the lectern, and the marshal sets the time clock to thirty minutes. It starts to count down, but she just stands there. Mom and Dad each give her a thumbs-up, but that doesn't help. She looks at me, and I give her this begging-little-brother look. That doesn't help either.

Chief Justice Reynolds clears his throat and nods at the clock, which is down to 29:30 and counting. How much more of our time is she going to waste?!

She's practically dripping sweat from her upper lip. But it's not anger sweat this time. It's terror sweat.

Down to 28:50 . . . I give her a look—not like, *You can do this, Sadie; I believe in you,* but more like, *Come on, already!*

Then I elbow her hard in the arm.

She takes a deep breath and turns to the bench. I go

and sit down, this time at the appellants' table—in case she needs another elbow.)

SADIE WARREN: Mr. Chief Justice, and may it please the Court, this, um—

(That word again. But she takes a minute. She thinks it through.)

This is a case about the rights of children to have a childhood. We come before you because one sixth-grade boy, my brother, stood up for that right by refusing to do his homework. As you've seen in the days leading up to this hearing, over a million school-age children and their parents have stood with us to ask that you put an end to a practice that not only violates our nation's Constitution but harms its future.

JUSTICE RAUCH: How is homework harmful to the country's future?

SADIE WARREN: There's too much of it, Justice Rauch. Most of it is quite dull. It takes away the downtime, the dream time, if you will, of the next generation's developing minds.

JUSTICE DEFAZIO: I thought that homework was designed

to reinforce what was covered in class. A ten- or fifteen-minute exercise.

SADIE WARREN: It may have been once upon a time, Justice DeFazio. But the fact is, today's teachers are so stressed by Common Core and the high-stakes testing that goes with it, they use homework to get done what they can't do in class.

JUSTICE FITZGERALD: What's wrong with that?

SADIE WARREN: It doesn't work, for one thing. Kids are too burnt out by the time they get home. The evidence shows that in elementary school, homework has a negative impact on student outcomes. In middle school it's neutral. And in high school there may be a slight advantage, but at a great cost.

JUSTICE SUERTE: Cost to what?

SADIE WARREN: Childhood.

JUSTICE RAUCH: How can we be sure that this homework epidemic, which you imply plagues the youth, is real? Where's the proof?

SADIE WARREN: We included several homework surveys in our brief, Justice Rauch.

JUSTICE RENFRO: Kids might exaggerate their answers on the survey. We need empirical evidence.

UNIDENTIFIED BOY FROM VISITORS' SECTION: You want evidence? Take a look at this.

(Alistair jumps up and approaches the nine robed justices. The marshal blocks his way. But Alistair does a quick fake left and then steps right to get around him. He rolls up his left sleeve and continues.)

Math book pages forty-five to fifty, odds *and* evens. *Plus* worksheet on decimals.

(He rolls up his right.)

World History. Read chapter four. Do Skills Practice on page eighty-seven.

(He pulls up his shirt.)

Figure out how many steps it took for a forty-niner to walk from Missouri to California. Gimme a break! She doesn't even say how big the guy's feet are.

(He pulls up his shirt even more. Now he's reading upside down.)

Spelling test on Friday. Geography quiz Monday. Finish *Black Ships Before Troy* by Tuesday. Oh, and this reminder about my science project.

   . (He yanks his shirt all the way over his head and—heaven help us!—flashes the United States Supreme Court. Across his chest he wrote "Solar Power.")

And that's just one weekend!

CHIEF JUSTICE REYNOLDS: Please, don't show us another.

(The time clock is down to seventeen minutes.)

SADIE WARREN: Furthermore, we find that homework is a health hazard. The American Academy of Pediatrics recommends sixty minutes of vigorous daily exercise to combat childhood obesity, which has tripled in this country since 1960. Homework is just another sedentary activity that lasts one to four hours a day.

JUSTICE ROSENBURG: Don't they have PE anymore?

SADIE WARREN: Yes, Justice Rosenburg, but the physical education programs have been severely cut back. Many schools offer it only once a week.

JUSTICE FITZGERALD: What about recess?

SADIE WARREN: Recess is used as a privilege by some teachers and is taken away when students don't turn in their homework.

JUSTICE RAUCH: Your concern about the health hazards seems to be far-fetched.

UNIDENTIFIED BOY FROM VISITORS' SECTION: No way is it far-fetched! Take a look at this!

(Alistair drags his backpack up and plops it on the marble floor in front of the bench.)

My backpack. I brought it all the way from Los Angeles to show you. Had to pay an excess baggage fee at the airport. Every day I drag this thing to school and back home again. It gives me a crick in the neck. Not to mention the long-term damage I imagine it's doing to my spine. And I'm not the only one. Kids all over the country carry this much and more. They're weighing in on our website. Sean, what's the national total up to?

OTHER UNIDENTIFIED BOY FROM VISITORS' SECTION: 230,456,474 pounds on the backs of school children across America.

UNIDENTIFIED BOY FROM VISITORS' SECTION: If that's not cruel and unusual punishment, what is?

(There is another pause. This time it's the justices who are speechless.)

SADIE WARREN: Thank you, Alistair. Besides the bodily damage it does, homework has a negative impact on emotional health, too. If you could visit the homes of school-age children after school, you'd hear small fists pounding tables in frustration. You'd smell coffee being brewed by eleven-year-olds desperate to study for one more test, complete one more task. And you'd see bedside clocks showing one a.m. next to empty beds, where teenagers should be sleeping, but instead they're hunched over desks, battling a deadline.

(She waits for another pitch, but none comes.)

SADIE WARREN: Moving on, if I may, to a purely legal argument, there is also the privacy question.

(We all look over at Justice DeFazio now.)

We accept that kids have to go to school. It's the law, and it gives them the benefit of an education—

JUSTICE COHEN: While allowing their parents to work.

SADIE WARREN: Yes, Justice Cohen, but we feel that just as their parents get off work at, say, five or six o'clock, students should have away time too. And that away time should be free of intrusion by the state. In this case, the schools.

JUSTICE RAUCH: Parents take work home. Some of them work all the time. That's the nature of a competitive society. Shouldn't we prepare our children for it?

SADIE WARREN: Parents are paid to do the work they bring home, Justice Rauch. Kids are just pressured to do it. If they don't, they get punished or publicly shamed by teachers who post homework charts in class.

JUSTICE FITZGERALD: Are you saying that there's no benefit at all to homework?

SADIE WARREN: None proven, Justice Fitzgerald. And that does raise the question, if kids aren't being paid to do the work, and there's no proof that the work benefits them, then whom does it benefit? The real estate industry, which enjoys higher home values in neighborhoods with homework-heavy schools? The pharmaceutical industry, which has seen prescriptions for ADHD and anxiety drugs rise at the exact same rate as homework has risen? With so many hours of unpaid work for the benefit of others, then, we believe that homework is itself a violation of child labor laws.

(I check the clock: eleven minutes left.)

SADIE WARREN: Also, if you look to common law principles to support our claim, you'll find that in 2009 the Supreme Court of Canada granted one family the right to refuse homework for their son.

(Justice Fitzgerald makes a note on a pad.)

JUSTICE COHEN: The examples you cite in your brief, of endless worksheets and online exercises, do seem like a poor use of children's time. But surely not all homework is as mind numbing as that.

SADIE WARREN: It's true that some teachers are more creative and challenge their students to think. But they don't have time. They're too busy rushing to complete the standards. And they're under the same pressure kids are to boost test scores.

(Eight minutes.)

SADIE WARREN: I also hope you'll consider the Fourteenth Amendment's guarantee of equal protection under the law. In 1954 this Court found that racially segregated schools were inherently unequal. But there's another inequality that hasn't been addressed, and that's the socioeconomic inequality. During the school day, students sit together, they play together, they learn together. But then they go home—some to an empty home because both parents work, others to a home full of advantages like college-educated moms and dads, technology, and tutors. By giving homework, then, the schools are forcing students back into a condition of separate, unequal, and therefore unconstitutional education.

JUSTICE ROSENBURG: Shouldn't all kids be doing their homework alone?

JUSTICE FITZGERALD: I did.

JUSTICE DEFAZIO: I did.

JUSTICE RENFRO: I did.

JUSTICE SUERTE: I did.

CHIEF JUSTICE REYNOLDS: Had help.

JUSTICE COHEN: Mom was a teacher. Had help.

JUSTICE RAUCH: Mom and Dad were lawyers. No help.

(The justices all lean forward to look at Justice Williams, but he just rolls his eyes. The court clock turns white: two minutes left.)

JUSTICE RENFRO: So, to be fair to the less fortunate, then, we should abolish homework and expand the school day?

(Sadie freezes. The whole courtroom goes silent. All the kids start to panic.)

SADIE WARREN: No.

JUSTICE RENFRO: And why not?

(The light on the clock turns red: one minute. Sadie looks at me. It's really just a glance, but it eats up ten seconds. Then she looks back at the bench.)

SADIE WARREN: For the same reason we have come before you today. A child born in the United States in 1900 could expect to live fifty, maybe fifty-five years. That same child born today will likely live to eighty or eighty-five, maybe much longer. This Court has always relied on the test of reason for its decisions. I ask you, how is it reasonable that, when we've made the human lifespan longer, we're making childhood shorter? You all had free time when you were kids. Chief Justice Reynolds, you were on the wrestling team in high school. That made you tough—and not just in the ring. Justice Cohen, you reread *Pride and Prejudice* every year. Not because you had to for a class, but because it was your favorite book. Justice Suerte, you were a Yankees fan. I'll bet you learned a lot of math just from keeping track of their stats. And if you hadn't had free time to watch *Perry Mason*, would you have fallen in love with the law? And you, Justice Rauch, you grew up in Colorado, one of our nation's most beautiful states. Think about the time you spent outdoors. Wasn't that a part of your education? Mr. Chief Justice, and may it please the Court, you have the power to make a sea change in the lives of young people today. Give us back our childhoods. Give us the freedom to follow our own interests, to be curious again, to dream, and to have time to spend with our friends, our parents and grandparents, and our little brothers and sisters. Give us, as only you can, the ultimate homework pass: end it for all time.

(You know how I said the Supreme Court is as quiet as a cathedral? Not now, it isn't. There's cheering from the audience and the press. Cheering for my big sister.)

CHIEF JUSTICE REYNOLDS: Thank you, Miss Warren.

(The clerk resets the clock. There's no time for the bathroom or snacks or even to breathe because here comes Livingston Gulch.)

TRANSCRIPT

ORAL ARGUMENT ON BEHALF OF THE RESPONDENTS

CHIEF JUSTICE REYNOLDS: Mr. Gulch?

(Livingston Gulch stands, his hands tucked into the pockets of his green jacket. As he and Sadie walk past each other, he nods at her. He steps to the lectern and stands there in a long silence even though the Supreme Court clock is already counting down from 30:00. He stays perfectly still until the clock hits 29:30, and the first words step out of Gulch's mouth.)

LIVINGSTON GULCH: *Loco.* Mr. Chief Justice, and may it please the Court, this is a case of *in loco parentis.* For those of you who don't do your homework, that's Latin for "in place of the parents." It's been the cornerstone of public education since the very first day of school. Society has given—and this Court has upheld—the right of the school boards to act in the best interest of the students.

JUSTICE RENFRO: How's this a *loco parentis* case? Homework is supposed to be done at home.

LIVINGSTON GULCH: Well, Justice Renfro, it's precisely because so many parents are not at home after four that the schools need to extend *in loco parentis* into the evening hours. With homework. It keeps the latchkey kids out of trouble.

JUSTICE COHEN: What about the homes where there are tutors or educated parents to help? What do you say to Miss Warren's argument that this creates an equal protection violation?

LIVINGSTON GULCH: I say the same thing I noted in my brief. Libraries with free homework help are available to all who can't afford a tutor.

JUSTICE SUERTE: And you think that paves a level playing field in our nation's schools?

LIVINGSTON GULCH: The playing field will never be level in this country, Justice Suerte. It's not the American way.

Some will have to work harder to get across it, as I did by working my way through law school, and as you and your brother, Juan, did by studying the encyclopedia.

(He bugged our suite at the Watergate. He bugged us for sure!)

JUSTICE RENFRO: What if homework's not in the best interest of the child? What if, as Miss Warren suggests, it's akin to illegal child labor?

LIVINGSTON GULCH: Next thing you know she'll claim it's a violation of the Thirteenth Amendment.

JUSTICE WILLIAMS: That's not what she said.

(Huge gasp from the audience! Justice Williams just broke his longtime silence.)

LIVINGSTON GULCH: Sounded like she was going there to me, Justice Williams.

JUSTICE WILLIAMS: She said that the labor of homework benefits the real estate and pharmaceutical industries. And since children aren't being paid to do it, it violates the Fair Labor Standards Act. I'm intrigued by the argument.

CHIEF JUSTICE REYNOLDS: Why *are* we putting so much pressure on children, especially since, as Miss Warren pointed out, we're living longer than we used to?

LIVINGSTON GULCH: The trouble with her lifespan argument, Chief, is that children born today are going to have a harder time finding a job, because senior citizens—I'm not pointing any fingers, Justice Rosenburg—are taking longer to step down.

JUSTICE DEFAZIO: Does the state—in this case the schools—have the right to mandate behavior in people's homes?

LIVINGSTON GULCH: By that line of thinking, Justice DeFazio, people will say they don't have to fill out their tax returns. We've all got homework due on the fifteenth of April, don't we?

JUSTICE ROSENBURG: Surely the emotional health of a child is consistent with the pursuit of happiness, Mr. Gulch. Homework does seem to be taking away that right from our children.

LIVINGSTON GULCH: Pursuit of happiness is an adult's right, Justice Rosenburg, not a child's. First they have to be educated. Then they have to get jobs. Then they can pay for their happiness.

JUSTICE COHEN: Are you suggesting that this Court made a mistake when it ruled in *Tinker v. Des Moines* that students do not shed their constitutional rights at the schoolhouse gate?

JUSTICE RAUCH: Or *Goss v. Lopez* when it ruled that a child's rights can't be denied without due process?

JUSTICE RENFRO: Why should pursuit of happiness be any different from those rights?

LIVINGSTON GULCH: Would you trust a child to pursue his own happiness, Justice Renfro? If so, why not get rid of compulsory education altogether? Let kids anesthetize themselves in front of their beloved screens until they come of age.

JUSTICE SUERTE: You take an awfully dim view of today's youth, Mr. Gulch. Their pursuit of happiness might surprise you with its substance.

LIVINGSTON GULCH: And it might surprise you, Justice Suerte, with its emptiness. Eight- to eighteen-year-olds spend up to sixteen hours a day on screens. Seventy-six percent of teens use social media. Eighty-three percent of teenage boys play video games. Among teenage girls, the median number of text messages sent each day is fifty. They're texting,

Facebooking, Snapchatting, and Instagramming themselves into oblivion.

JUSTICE FITZGERALD: What about common law precedent? What do you say about the Supreme Court of Canada upholding a family's right to refuse homework?

LIVINGSTON GULCH: Canada. Not China. You don't see the hard-working nations of this planet coddling their youth.

JUSTICE RAUCH: Isn't there a benefit to allowing kids time in nature without the constant pressures of schoolwork?

LIVINGSTONE GULCH: You might find God in a trout stream, Justice Rauch. But I doubt you'll find a good-paying job there.

(Gulch's clock turns red. He has one minute left.)

Which brings me to my final point. It's true that children are the future of any nation. So consider this as you consider the future of ours. Compared with students in other countries, American students score thirty-first in math, seventeenth in reading, and twenty-third in science. In all three categories, China scored number one. Do you think kids in China are complaining about their homework? Do you think kids in Korea are worried about the pursuit of happiness? No. They're too busy pursuing excellence.

Mr. Chief Justice, and may it please the Court, from where you sit, you are obligated to take the long view. Back to our founders, who left matters of education up to individual states and school boards. Ahead to our future, a nation of people ill prepared to compete in the global job market. This is no time to overstep your limits and disarm our teachers in the war on mediocrity. Let them use every weapon they have to make America great again. Including homework. I yield the balance of my time.

JUSTICE ROSENBURG: I wonder if we might hear from the boy who brought the case. Sam, in your own words, can you tell us why you're here?

(Okay, I told you I have a hard time talking to grown-ups. But in front of *these* grownups I'm terrified. Not only are they the Supreme Court of the United States, but they're floating high above me on thrones. The Guided Meditation Lady whispers in my head, *Things can be accomplished in a calm, relaxed way, so breathe.* I picture Mr. Kalman on the ground and refusing to say uncle to big Joe Mancuso. And I swallow an advice pill from Bernice. *You can't tear down a wall if you don't take a swing.* So I swing.)

SAM WARREN: I'm here, Justice Rosenburg, because I couldn't take it anymore. I go to school all day. I work hard. I do what I'm told. I don't complain. And I'm definitely not a crybaby. I like school. We learn a lot there. But when I finally get home, the last thing I want to do is more schoolwork. I want to run around, play the piano, see my friends. I want to draw and build a treehouse and learn what I want to learn. The way Steve Jobs did when he was a kid. The way Benjamin Franklin and Bill Gates and Herbie Hancock did when they were kids. Earlier this year we had to do projects on endangered species. I did mine on the red panda because I love trees and so do they. But if I had to do it over again, I'd choose a different endangered species. I'd choose childhood.

CHIEF JUSTICE REYNOLDS: Thank you, Sam. In light of the national attention this case has drawn, and the size of the crowd outside today, I'm ordering the clerk to set aside all pending matters so that we may go directly into conference. The case is submitted.

23

WHAT HAPPENED TO MR. KALMAN

On our way back to the hotel, Sadie says we have to plan Mr. Kalman's funeral.

"Mr. Kalman died?" Catalina's lower lip starts to quiver.

"Let's not jump to conclusions," Dad says. "We don't know what happened to him."

"Well, if he's not dead yet," Sadie says, "he will be as soon as I get my hands on him."

We hop out of our cabs, and the doorman says, "If you're looking for Mr. Kalman, I'm afraid they took him to George Washington University Hospital."

We all get real quiet. The quiet of a little kid who just dropped his toy but isn't sure if it's broken or not. The quiet before you cry.

We jump back into the cabs.

All eight of us march into the emergency room at George

Washington University Hospital. A woman in the waiting area coughs.

"Maybe we should wait outside," Alistair says, ducking behind Dad. "You can catch nasty diseases in an ER."

"Sadie, why don't you take Sam in? If Mr. Kalman wants a visit, he'll want it from you. Just text us as soon as you know what's going on," Dad says.

There are certain things in life that kids have a hard time doing. And I don't mean little things like tying shoelaces. I'm talking about big things—driving a car, joining the army, or having a beer. You can't do any of those until you're sixteen, eighteen, or twenty-one. They're good restrictions because they keep us and other people safe.

But suppose a kid wants to visit someone in the hospital. You can't unless you're thirteen or older. In rare instances, they'll make an exception for family.

This is one rule I just don't get. The point of being in a hospital is what? To get sicker? No, it's to get well. And what better medicine is there than a visit from kids? I mean, what do they think we're planning to do, run through the halls of the emergency room playing tag and spreading whooping cough? I told you already, kids get it. We know to be quiet here. We know to wash our hands with the disinfectant by the door. And we'd never come if we had a cold.

But the nurse at the nurses' station doesn't trust us.

When Sadie and I tell her we're here to see Mr. Kalman, she gives us this *I'm-in-charge-and-you're-not* look.

"Are you family?" she asks.

"Neighbors."

"You can't visit him unless you're at least thirteen."

"She's eighteen," I say. "Today's her birthday."

"What about you?"

"I'll be twelve in March."

She points to a sign: ALL VISITORS MUST BE AT LEAST 13 YEARS OF AGE. RARE EXCEPTIONS MADE FOR FAMILY MEMBERS.

Now, when Mr. Hill wants to end a conversation, he stands up from his chair, and that's your cue to leave. But this nurse is already standing, so she ends it by putting her reading glasses back on and looking at somebody's chart.

"I'm his *prochain ami*," I say.

Her reading glasses stay on but her eyes come up over the top like a couple of early morning suns.

"His what?"

"*Prochain ami*," I explain. "That's French for 'next friend.' It's a legal term. I'm surprised you don't know it."

"It means," Sadie says, "that their relationship is equivalent to family for all legal purposes—including hospital visitation rights. Does your employee contract give you immunity from lawsuits?"

Here's where the reading glasses come off and dangle on the chain around her neck.

"I don't think so."

"Want to risk it?"

It's a total staring contest right now between Sadie and the nurse with no reading glasses. Then I see a flash of fear in those rising suns.

"He's in room six," the nurse with no reading glasses says, "down that hall."

Sadie sweeps aside the curtain. Mr. Kalman is lying propped up in a bed, his eyes closed. He's wearing a hospital gown, and his legs are under a thin blanket. I can see wires running from under the gown to a monitor the size of an iPad. It's got an odd screen saver—a line with little *V*s running through it—like one of the first video games. The room is quiet except for a *bleep* coming from one of the machines.

"Well, at least we know he's not dead," I say, because I've guessed correctly that the bleeping sound is his heartbeat.

"Mr. Kalman?" Sadie says.

He opens his eyes.

"Call me Avi, please. Here of all places. And at such a time."

"Avi," she says. "What happened to you?"

"I had a fall. One minute I was outside, getting some air, and the next I was on the ground, passed out. Someone called 911, and the paramedics brought me here."

I can see that Sadie's really worried about him now. All that talk about his funeral . . . she didn't mean it.

"What did the doctor say? Are you going to be all right?"

"They're running some tests. Pictures of the head. Pictures of the heart. I tried to tell them both are fine, but they wouldn't listen. Doctors and lawyers don't mix."

He sits up, and you can tell something's giving him pain. I'm worried it's his hip. He points to a glass of water on the wheelie table nearby.

"Would you mind, Sadie? It hurts to reach."

She grabs the water and holds it to his mouth. He takes a sip, then nods that he's had enough.

"So," he says, "did we postpone the case?"

Sadie and I look at each other.

"Postpone?" she says.

"Didn't you get my text?"

"What text?"

"From the ambulance I texted you, 'Under the circumstances, Chief Justice Reynolds, we'd like to postpone.'"

"I never got that," Sadie says.

"What do you mean you never got it? It's right here on my phone."

Mr. Kalman holds up a cell phone. On the screen, just as he said, are the words *Under the circumstances, Chief Justice Reynolds, we'd like to postpone.*

"Did you press 'send'?" Sadie asks.

"Yes," Mr. Kalman says. "At least I think so."

"Avi, you didn't! The text never got sent."

"So we didn't postpone?"

Sadie and I both shake our heads.

"Who argued the case?"

I point to Sadie.

"You? But you're not even a member of the Supreme Court Bar."

"I am now! I paid the two hundred dollars!"

They look at each other for a second. Then Sadie gets all flushed. "Wait a minute," she says. "This is all a joke, isn't it?"

"There's nothing funny about a fall, Sadie. I could have broken my hip."

"But the two hundred dollars. You put it in my pocket because you knew they'd ask for it."

"Why would the Supreme Court want to take your birthday money?"

"Because that's the fee for joining the Bar!"

"Really?" he says. "It's gone up. I paid only a hundred."

Now Sadie's face is all confused.

"This isn't a joke?" she says.

Mr. Kalman shakes his head. Then he looks at me.

"She really argued in front of the Supreme Court?"

I nod. "She really did."

"The case is submitted?"

We both nod. Mr. Kalman can hardly believe it.

"I guess you turned eighteen just in time."

24

THE SUPREME COURT RULES

If you look on PocketJustice, you'll see that most Supreme Court cases take months to get decided. A case argued in, say, October won't be decided until January of the next year — or later.

Brown v. Board of Education, for example, was argued in December 1953 but didn't get decided until May 1954.

But there are exceptions. *Bush v. Gore,* for instance, when the two presidential candidates were fighting about which votes to count in the 2000 election, was argued on December 11 and decided on December 12, the very next day.

That's because it was a case "of vital interest to the nation." You can't exactly have no president, can you?

And you can't exactly have a hundred thousand kids camped out on the sidewalk in front of the Supreme Court when they're supposed to be in school. If they're not in school, their parents can't be at work. And if their parents can't be at work, that's a lot of people not doing their jobs. And if a lot of people aren't doing their jobs, it's horrible for the economy. And since the justices of the Supreme Court get paid from tax money that comes from people doing their jobs, you can see why when Alistair says, "How long could this take?" and Jaesang says, "They decided *Bush v. Gore* in one day," we think maybe it won't be so long, after all.

"That's good," Alistair says. "Because it's colder than a Sub-Zero out here and I don't think I could survive much longer, even with my extra body fat."

We wait all the rest of Monday. At four o'clock the bronze doors open and the marshal steps out. He shakes his head to let us know: no decision.

We're back at ten a.m. Tuesday. At noon the bronze doors open, the marshal steps out, and he shakes his head again. No decision.

At four he comes out again. Still no decision.

Wednesday morning the crowd is even bigger. It spills across the street and into the park. Our fingers are exhausted from playing games on our phones. No one can concentrate much on anything else. To make matters worse, at eleven o'clock it starts to snow.

By eleven-thirty I can't see my shoes anymore. If you were flying over the Supreme Court in a helicopter right now, you'd look down and think it was a miniature forest, the people huddled together like trees, their arms and heads all dusted white.

It's so quiet, and so white, that you might not notice the bronze doors opening. You might not notice the tall hat of the marshal, not turning side to side again, but this time nodding up and down.

They've reached a decision.

Soon there are footprints through the snow, and then a path up to the Supreme Court steps.

Before we head in, I stop and turn to Alistair, Jaesang, Catalina, Sadie, and Sean. "Guys," I say, "even if we don't get five or more on our side, what we've done here is pretty awesome. And we did it as a team."

We put our hands in the center. We don't raise them up in a cheer. We just leave them there for a second, holding on.

Then Catalina says, "To Mr. Kalman."

"To Mr. Kalman," we all say, and our hands fly up like birds.

Mr. Kalman said his test results were all fine, by the way. They sent him back to the hotel in a wheelchair. He has to keep his arm immobilized in a sling, but he should be okay. He's waiting for us at the suite, and he made us promise to come right over because he wants to hear the verdict from us and nobody else.

Inside the courtroom, Alistair says, "Same seats."

Sadie takes my hand and tugs me up to the appellants' table, where we stand together, still holding hands like we're about to see the Wizard of Oz. And we keep holding hands as the marshal of the court says, "Oyez, oyez, oyez! All persons having business before the Honorable, the Supreme Court of the United States, are admonished to draw near and give their attention, for the court is now sitting. God save the United States and this Honorable Court."

"He said to draw near," Catalina says. "Let's go."

Sean and Catalina and Jaesang and Alistair all crowd around Sadie and me. The justices come out from behind the red velvet curtain. They sit on their thrones. And just like before, the last one out is the Chief.

"Thank you, Marshal. In the case of *Warren v. Board of Education*, this court has reached a decision, a synopsis of which I will now read."

But first he looks up at Sadie and me, and I can't tell if it's a look of solidarity because we won, or sympathy because we lost. Then he reads out loud.

"The Board of Education asserts that its right to give homework is justified by its monumental task: to educate our children. We agree that this is a difficult task. As counsel noted, our students consistently rank far from the top in international assessments of math, science, and reading. Clearly, much work needs to be done to improve our nation's schools. Perhaps they need to reimagine not just what to teach, but how.

"The issue at hand, however, is whether or not we should limit the reach of the classroom into the home. Just as students do not shed their constitutional rights at the schoolhouse gate, neither do they shed those rights at their own front doors. Childhood is, as we've heard so ably argued here, a time of wonder, of curiosity, and of dreams. A society that cuts short that time by intruding into the private lives of children and their families may be risking its own demise. If childhood is, in fact, an endangered species, then this court asserts its duty to protect it from extinction. In the matter of *Warren v. Board of Education*, we side with the plaintiff, Sam Warren. The lower courts are overturned."

Sadie looks at me. "Sam, do you understand what he just said?"

"I think so," I say.

I turn and walk down the great aisle. I go through the lobby. I push open the heavy doors and look out at the crowd. Over a thousand people are waiting to hear from me.

So I take a deep breath and shout out to the crowd, to the sky, and to the future: *"The Supreme Court rules! No more homework! Ever!!!!!!"*

You could be an astronaut on the moon or an angel in heaven, and I swear you wouldn't miss the cheer that rises from the plaza. And if you were part of the crowd, you'd see, well, a whole lot of hugging. There's Jaesang and Catalina jumping up and down like two pogo sticks stuck together.

A three-way hug: Sean and Sadie and me in the middle.

Mom and Dad hugging like they're ten years younger.

Sean and Sadie like they're ten years older.

Alistair finally comes running out. "Wait, what? We won?"

"We won," I say. That's Alistair for you. It takes him a little longer to catch up, but when he does, you'd better hold on tight.

He grabs me and we do a double Truffle Shuffle, then throw our arms around each other and spin.

Then we all change places. Sadie and Mom with Dad in the middle. Jaesang, Catalina, and me. Alistair and Sean.

We change places *again*. This time I end up in Sadie's arms. We hug and spin and hug and spin, and neither one of us wants to let go.

"Thank you, Sadie. Thank you, Sadie. Thank you, Sadie," I say.

I open my eyes and see Livingston Gulch hovering nearby, like a gentleman about to ask for the next dance.

He raises his hand. Sadie calls on him. "Yes, Mr. Gulch?"

"If you ever need a job," he says, handing her his business card. And he walks off.

Dad comes up, and now *he* hugs Sadie.

"Somewhere in heaven," he says, "there's a proud mom."

Sadie looks over his shoulder at Mom.

"Here too," she says.

Soon we're all tangled up in one last hug.

You've heard of a poker face? You wear one when you play cards, like a mask, so the other players can't tell if you're bluffing.

Sadie and I learned the poker face from our dad, who learned it from his dad, who learned it from his. So it's kind of a Warren family tradition that whether you're holding a full house, a lousy pair of threes, or a secret, you keep it hidden behind your poker face.

Right now we're holding a royal flush.

Mr. Kalman is sitting in his wheelchair, eating a nice room service lunch in the Homework Suite, when we come to tell him the news. As soon as we step in, he pushes aside his sandwich and untucks the napkin from his shirt.

"I told the hotel staff no calls, no talk. I wanted to hear it straight from you."

We sit on the little settee, Sadie on one side and me on the other.

Sadie sighs and shakes her head. "It was seven to two."

"Who were the two?"

"Renfro and Rauch."

"Not Williams?"

"Williams voted with the majority."

"To . . . ?"

"To overturn the lower courts and declare homework unconstitutional!"

Mr. Kalman pumps the air with his fist. Sadie throws her arms around him and starts crying joyful tears.

Hey, that's an oxymoron!

But there ought to be a different word for it. The "moron" part makes it sound dumb. And there's nothing dumb about laughing and crying at the same time. She's just been hold-ing back the tears until there was some laughter to balance them out.

"Seven to two!" Mr. Kalman says. "And Williams on our side!"

He shakes his head, smiling. That's a paradox — the yes and no of it, the *I can't believe it but I know it's true.*

And then, because he can't contain his joy, the old man leaps out of the wheelchair, rips off his sling and tosses it into the air, and starts swinging me around and around, dancing and jumping and pumping his arm like, well, like someone who *didn't* have a fall two days ago.

Mr. Kalman's poker face is even better than ours.

This is one time I'm a step ahead of my big sister. Because while Sadie has this crinkly look on her face, I'm shaking my head and smiling. Clever Mr. Kalman . . . he tricked us.

Pretty soon Sadie's crinkles turn to a frown, the frown to fire. Her eyes go wide and her upper lip starts to sweat.

Anger sweat, volcano style.

"I'm going to *kill you!*"

She takes a step toward Mr. Kalman like she's about to take a swing. But he puts his hand on her arm and looks her straight in the eye.

"*You* were their last, best hope," he says.

No oxymoron now. This time she's all tears.

EPILOGUE

Before *Warren v. Board of Education,* a typical Sunday afternoon in the life of a kid would go something like this: homework. More homework. One-eighth of one-quarter of one game of NFL football on TV. Back to homework. Dinner but not much appetite because of a swirly feeling in the stomach from dread of more homework. More homework. Bath. Brush teeth. Bed. Anxiety dream that you forgot to do your homework.

After *Warren v. Board of Education,* a typical Sunday afternoon goes like this: swirly feeling in your stomach, only now it's from soaring high on a swing set at the park.

There's probably a soccer practice going on at the same park. The whole team shows up, including Sean. He's a little out of shape, but not for long.

Nearby, under a tree, Catalina is jumping rope and

practicing for the pi contest: "3.1415926535 8979323846 2643383279 5028841971 6939937510 5820974944 5923078164 0628620899 8628034825 3421170679 8214808651 3282306647 0938446095 5058223172 5359408128 4811174502 8410270193 8521105559 6446229489 5493038196 4428810975 6659334461 2847564823 3786783165 2712019091 4564856692 3460348610 4543266482 1339360726 0249141273 7245870066 0631558817 4881520920 9628292540 9171536436 7892590360 0113305305 4882046652 1384146951 9415116094 3305727036 5759591953 0921861173 8193261179 3105118548 0744623799 6274956735 1885752724 8912279381 8301194912 9833673362 4406566430 8602139494 6395224737 1907021798 6094370277."

Those eighth-grade boys don't have a prayer.

Across town, in a gym, Alistair is sweating so much that all his old reminders are being washed away. After our trip to Washington, he decided that, like the Chief, he wants to be a wrestling champ. He's not giving up on *MasterChef*, though. "If all else fails," he told me, "I can fall back on my red velvets."

At Staples Center, Jaesang and his grandfather are cheering for the Lakers—in Korean.

In the teen zone, Sadie and Sean are enjoying their constitutional right to privacy. They're talking. Or kissing. Or maybe both.

And in the big oak tree in our backyard, I'm building a treehouse with my dad.

On the weekends, I go over to Mr. Kalman's house, where we answer the flood of mail we've been getting since the Supreme Court ruled.

One kid from North Dakota writes,

> DEAR MR. KALMAN,
>
> TODAY DAD AND I WENT HUNTING, AND I GOT MY VERY FIRST DEER. LAST SEASON I WASN'T ALLOWED TO GO. TOO MUCH HOMEWORK. THANKS TO YOU, NOW I'M FREE.
>
> YOURS TRULY,
> DOUGLAS FRASIER.

"Hope you got him in one shot, Doug," Mr. Kalman says as he starts to write back.

One of those letters was addressed to me.

> Dear Sam,
>
> You and your headstrong sister brought an old man back to life. Thank you for changing me to a better channel.
>
> Your neighbor and friend,
> Avi Kalman

That night, as I'm getting ready for bed, I tap the meditation app on my phone. Tap and hold, that is. Then I drag it up to the trashcan.

"Are you sure you want to delete?" the Guided Meditation Lady asks.

I tap "yes."

On March 14, Catalina stuns the school by reciting 947 digits of pi. Her nearest challenger is an eighth-grade boy who makes it all the way to 207.

A week later, Sean travels to Sacramento for the state Academic Decathlon championship. We watch online as the final question in the varsity, or C-student category, is read aloud: "This Latin legal term meaning 'a formal order asking to be more informed or be made certain' is what the Supreme Court grants when it agrees to take a lower court's case on appeal.

"(a) habeas corpus
"(b) *de minimis non curat lex*
"(c) caveat emptor
"(d) writ of certiorari
"(e) none of the above.

"Ten seconds."

Mr. Kalman grins. Sadie laughs. Alistair and Jaesang elbow me from either side. Catalina swings her braid.

When the ten seconds are up, the announcer asks for the answer cards.

Sean is the only one holding up (d) writ of certiorari.

Our cheer is holding up the sky.

One day at the end of the month, while sitting with Dad on the couch and checking her email, Sadie screams really loud: "I got into Harvard? Princeton? Yale? I didn't even apply to those schools!"

Turns out she had some letters of recommendation she didn't know about.

From nine men and women in a very high place.

In June we have our stepping-up ceremony at school. Mr. Trotter brings the orchestra onstage, and we play a jazz combo with the wooden xylophones and some African drums. He asked me if I wanted to do a piano solo, but I said no, thanks. I just wanted to play with everyone else.

Afterward we all go back to Mr. Kalman's house for lunch. The path to his front door is sunny now. The doorbell doesn't stick.

"Hey, Alistair," I say when he gets there with his mom and dad, "I got you an end-of-the-year present."

"For me? For real?"

"Go ahead. Open it."

He's expecting a pack of Post-its or a planner, but what he unwraps is—

"The panda! Seriously?"

"I even signed the tag for you."

"But I went back for it. It wasn't there."

"It *was* there. You forgot where you hid it."

"Behind the cooking magazine, I thought."

"Fishing."

"Man, I should've written that down. Thanks, Sam. I hope we can spend lots of time together this summer."

"Me too," I tell him.

"That is, if you're not sick of seeing me on TV."

"TV? You're going to be on TV?"

"Yup. I tried out for the next season of *MasterChef Junior*. Made it onto the show."

"You're kidding! Wow, Alistair. That's amazing! I'm so happy for you."

"Know what convinced the judges? I whipped up some of Mr. Kalman's tuna salad. I'm forever indebted to that man."

Aren't we all?

Mr. Kalman tells Jaesang it's time for them to conduct business. He calls him over to the dining room table, where we all worked so hard to plan our case. The legal papers are gone now; it's just a big buffet of food. But there's enough room on one corner for Jaesang to set his three-ring binder full of basketball cards.

Mr. Kalman offers the terms.

"Oldest for youngest."

"What do you mean?"

"You give me the current Lakers starting lineup."

"For?"

"The 1972 NBA champs — if I can find them all in this drawer."

Mr. Kalman slides open the bottom drawer of his antique wooden hutch. He doesn't just slide it open; he pulls it all the way out and carries it over to the dining room table, sets it down, and starts poking through it with his finger. Pretty soon he's pulling out basketball cards that are more than forty years old. They'd be worth thousands on Ebay.

Jaesang can't help leaning closer and closer to each card.

Gail Goodrich, number 25.

Happy Hairston, number 52.

Elgin Baylor, 22.

Jerry West, 44.

Jaesang's eyes are getting as big as basketballs. To him, collecting all five of the starting Lakers from 1972 would be like winning the lottery.

He's got four out of five. He needs one more card.

"Say, Mr. Kalman," he says, trying to sound all casual, "you don't happen to have a Wilt Chamberlain in the bunch, do you?"

Wilt the Stilt Chamberlain, lucky number 13, one of the all-time greats in the NBA. He led the Lakers to a thirty-three-game winning streak in the 1971–72 season. And he once scored over 100 points in a single game!

Jaesang has been searching all his life for a 1972 Wilt Chamberlain. That's the year the Lakers beat Boston four games to one in the NBA finals.

Mr. Kalman's finger fishes around some more. He turns over the faces of NBA greats from the last century. John Havlicek . . . Walt Frazier . . . Julius Erving.

"Chamberlain, you say?"

"It would sort of complete the squad."

His bony finger flicks aside more cards. Then he picks one up and holds it close to his cloudy eyes.

"Here's one, but you can't see his jersey too well."

"Why not?"

Mr. Kalman drops the card face-up onto the table.

It's signed!

Jaesang drops face-up onto the floor. It takes Alistair's homemade cheesecake to revive him.

We're halfway through dessert when the doorbell rings. Mr. Kalman is busy brewing more coffee, so Dad answers for him.

Guess who walks in a second later?

Our teacher, Mr. Powell. He doesn't say hello. Just

stands in the entryway, a little awkward, until he can catch Mr. Kalman's eye.

"I want to sue the school board," he says.

"On what grounds?"

"On the grounds that standardized testing is unconstitutional."

"Where's the violation?"

"Teaching to the test deprives students of their right to a real education. And publishing the results violates teachers' privacy."

Mr. Kalman puts down the coffeepot and brings his hand to his forehead. It's not a headache or anything. He's just thinking.

He turns to Sean. "You in?"

"I can manage the website from Berkeley."

"Sam?"

"Sure. I hate those tests."

Catalina offers to figure out how much money the district wastes on testing. Alistair says he'll cater our meals while we work on the case. Jaesang's willing to sell some cards from his collection to help raise money. "But not the Chamberlain. I'm keeping that for college."

"What about you, Sadie? You in?"

"I'll FaceTime from my dorm," she says. "Yeah, I'm in."

Mr. Kalman turns to Mr. Powell. "We're all in. We'll take your case."

And that's just about the end of my story. Except for the hardest part of all. In August, when the treehouse is built and the summer is almost over, we drive Sadie and my dad to the airport. He's going to fly out with her to college and help her move into the dorm. I have to stay home to start seventh grade.

Which means Sadie and I are about to say goodbye.

The closer we get to the airport, the less we talk. My vocabulary has always been abridged, while Sadie's is usually the whole dictionary in one mouth. Not now, though. Now she's real quiet. We both are. And when the moment comes, we say things like "See ya," and "Yeah," and "Okay," and "Time to go, I guess." All other words get stuck in our throats.

But there are more of them that I wanted to say. So when I get home, I take a pen and a sheet of paper, and I write her a letter.

August 26

Dear Sadie,

After we watched you getting higher and higher on the escalator, and then higher and higher in the sky, Mom and I drove home. It was the quietest car ride ever.

I decided to make this letter the first thing I do as the only kid in the house. And I decided to write it in your room.

Which I barely recognize. You left all those pictures taped to the wall, of you and your debate team, and of Lucy and Mollie, and me and Dad, and our mom and your mom, and that selfie you took with Mr. Kalman and all of us on the steps of the Supreme Court.

But the floor of your room is totally transformed. Did your dirty dishes and laundry go away to college too?

Maybe when you're home for winter break, before you mess it up again, we can bring down the Playmobil.

Remember how you used to let me come into your room, and we'd make up stories and then turn them into stop-motion movies?

What I wanted to tell you at the airport but couldn't because I was feeling too sad to talk, is that in those stories we made up, the big sister always saved the little brother.

In real life, she did too.

Love,

Sam

P.S. I just thought of another oxymoron. It's one that used to keep me up at night, but now it's just a memory.

Homework.

GLOSSARY OF LEGAL TERMS

APPEALS COURT A court to which a dissatisfied party may appeal a decision.

APPELLANT A person or party who appeals a lawsuit.

APPELLEE A person or party in whose favor a previous decision is being appealed.

BRIEF A written document used to present an argument in court.

CIRCUIT COURT A higher appeals court. There are thirteen federal circuit courts as part of the judicial branch of government.

CLAIMANT A person filing a claim for damage.

Class action suit A lawsuit in which the petitioner's case is used to settle all potential cases with the same claim.

De minimis non curat lex "The law does not concern itself with trifles."

Dissent A judge's written disagreement with the majority decision.

Docket The calendar of cases.

Federal court A court under the jurisdiction of the federal judiciary.

Hearing A formal presentation of a complaint at which all interested parties have an opportunity to respond.

In loco parentis "In place of the parents."

Kangaroo court A court thrown together at the last minute with no regard for justice.

Minor A person under the legal age of adulthood, usually eighteen or twenty-one.

Oyez, oyez, oyez "Hear ye, hear ye, hear ye." What the clerk of the Supreme Court says when the court is in session.

PETITIONER A person who brings a lawsuit.

PRO BONO "For good." A lawyer or law firm that takes a case pro bono does not charge for its services.

PRO HAC VICE "For this occasion only." A person who is not a member of the Supreme Court Bar but who is otherwise eligible may make arguments *pro hac vice.*

PROCHAIN AMI "Next friend." Even without their parents' permission, minors can sue if they have a *prochain ami,* or a grownup willing to file the suit for them.

RESPONDENT The person or entity that is being sued.

SUPREME COURT The highest court in the land. A decision by the Supreme Court is final unless overturned by a future Supreme Court.

WRIT OF CERTIORARI A formal request of the Supreme Court to hear a case.

APPENDIX OF SUPREME COURT CASES MENTIONED IN THIS BOOK

A.M. v. Holmes Upheld the arrest of a thirteen-year-old boy for fake-burping in gym class. The Tenth Circuit Court of Appeals ruling was let stand by the Supreme Court.

Bethel School District v. Fraser Upheld the suspension of a student for obscene speech.

Board of Education v. Earls Gave schools the right to require drug testing of all students who participate in extracurricular activities (fictionalized here as *Lee v. Oklahoma School District*).

Brown v. Board of Education of Topeka, Kansas Unanimous decision that declared the doctrine of "separate but equal" unconstitutional.

BUSH V. GORE Held that the state of Florida's court-ordered manual recount of ballots in the 2000 presidential election was unconstitutional.

ENGEL V. VITALE Prohibited state-sponsored prayer at school.

EQUAL EMPLOYMENT OPPORTUNITY COMMISSION V. ABERCROMBIE & FITCH Protected job applicants from discriminatory dress codes.

GOSS V. LOPEZ Established education as a property right.

GRISWOLD V. CONNECTICUT Established a zone of privacy for married couples in the bedroom.

HAZELWOOD SCHOOL DISTRICT V. KUHLMEIER Gave principals the right to censor student-run newspapers.

HEDGEPETH V. WASHINGTON METROPOLITAN TRANSIT AUTHORITY Upheld the arrest of a twelve-year-old girl for eating a french fry.

HODGE V. TALKIN Lower court ruling that the Supreme Court let stand. Allowed a ban on speech and assembly on the plaza of the Supreme Court.

IN RE GAULT Established that minors have constitutional rights.

MIRANDA V. ARIZONA Protected the Fifth Amendment right to remain silent.

MORSE V. FREDERICK Gave schools the right to limit student speech if it is disruptive of school activities.

OBERGEFELL V. HODGES Gave same-sex couples the right to marry.

PIERCE V. SOCIETY OF SISTERS Upheld the right of states to regulate schools and to examine both teachers and pupils.

SANTA FE INDEPENDENT SCHOOL DISTRICT V. DOE Affirmed *Engel v. Vitale* against prayer in public schools.

TINKER V. DES MOINES INDEPENDENT SCHOOL DISTRICT Gave students the right to protest at school as long as they don't disrupt class.

WARREN V. BOARD OF EDUCATION Declared homework unconstitutional.

GRATITUDE

A book's origins often reach back to childhood. This one reaches back to my children's childhood, specifically to one evening during my daughter's third grade year when I heard an abrupt sound from the dining room table like twigs snapping. It was the logical, even-tempered eight-year-old Sophie Frank violently breaking number 2 pencils.

She couldn't solve Mr. Hall's weekly sudoku for homework.

So thank you, Sophie, for that uncharacteristic destruction of property; and thank you, Mr. Hall, for the age-inappropriate assignment. (She loved him, by the way, for his clarity and calm.)

And thank you, Sam, my son who drowned in homework at that same dining room table, mere feet from the piano he longed to play.

And thank you, Mia, my daughter who really did bring home a word search puzzle in which she had to find the word "school" forty-four times.

I'm also grateful to Alfie Kohn for his disruptive thinking about education so passionately offered in books like *The Homework Myth* and *Feel-Bad Education*.

To my fellow teachers who struggle with the idea of homework, not just because they have to grade it, but because they wonder if it really helps kids learn.

Gratitude again to my agent, Kevin O'Connor, whose enthusiasm and insight made the second draft almost as much fun as the first.

To Margaret Raymo, still a dream editor: I didn't have to break any pencils for you.

To Sharismar Rodriguez and Andy Smith for designing and drawing a cover that proclaims the power of kids with a cause.

Gratitude to my parents, Merona and Marty Frank, for being here.

To Julie Ferber Frank, a fierce advocate for the children in our home and the ones in this book. And for her wise contributions to the book itself.

Finally to you, Reader, for your gift of attention and time.

TURN THE PAGE TO CHECK OUT *ARMSTRONG & CHARLIE*,
ANOTHER CAN'T-MISS READ FROM STEVEN B. FRANK!

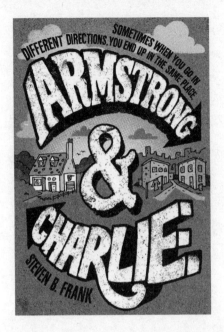

★ "[A] deeply moving and laugh-out-loud funny story
about family, friendship, integrity, and navigating
differences." —*KIRKUS REVIEWS*, starred review

"One of those distinctly American books that speaks
to us of who we are. . . . This novel is an exultation
of hope—and a dang good story to boot."
—*GARY SCHMIDT*, Newbery Honor–winning author of
The Wednesday Wars and *Okay for Now*

★ "One part comedy, one part poignant drama,
and one part food for thought."
—*SHELF AWARENESS*, starred review

· 1 ·

AN OPPORTUNITY

Charlie

"GUYS, WE SHOULD GO IN. It's a school night."

"Shut up, Charlie."

"Why'd you have to mention *that*?"

"Yeah, Killjoy Charlie. You just ended our summer vacation."

Like it's *my* fault the earth spins? I brace for a tornado of punches. Instead I hear Keith say, "Charlie Ross is right. It's getting dark."

Capture-the-flag ends in a tie and we all head for home. You can hear air conditioners humming from side yards and crickets chirping from trees. Someone kicks an empty Coke bottle into the street. It sounds like a ringing bell.

You can't hear much talk, though. We're all thinking about *you-know-what* starting *you-know-when*. Most summers I look forward to *you-know-what*. But this year I'm starting sixth grade. If I start sixth grade, chances are I'll finish it. And when I do, I'll get older than my older brother.

"See you guys at the bus stop tomorrow," I say.

"Won't see me," says Bobby Crane.

"Won't see me," says Mike Applebaum.

"Or me," says Brett Deitch.

"Why not?" I ask.

"I'm going to Buckley."

"I'm going to Carpenter."

"I'm going to El Rodeo."

Buckley is a private school in Sherman Oaks. Carpenter's a public one in Studio City. El Rodeo is in Beverly Hills.

That's three out of my four friends in the neighborhood changing schools. I turn to Keith, the one I look up to most.

"I'll see *you* at the bus stop, won't I, Keith?"

Keith has sandy blond hair, fair skin with freckles, and sea blue eyes. He carries a pocketknife in his jeans, started wearing puka shells way before they were popular, and lives in the pillow thoughts of practically every girl in Laurel Canyon. He calls us by our first and last names, which can make even a short kid like me feel tall.

"'Fraid not, Charlie Ross. I'm going to Carpenter this year. We gave my aunt's address in Studio City so I don't have to go to Wonderland."

"What's wrong with Wonderland?"

"My mom says it's going downhill."

"She say why?"

"Nope. Just that it's a good time to be movin' on. But don't worry, man. I'll still catch you around the neighborhood."

"Cool," I say, as in *No big deal.* But what I feel is cold. Like they all just ditched me.

Armstrong

The trouble with white people is, they're white. It's what I try to tell Mama when she informs me I'll be attending a new school.

"What's wrong with my old one?"

"It's segregated," Daddy says.

"How so? Black kids sit on one side of the schoolyard. Black kids on the other."

"And where do the white kids sit?"

"Only white kid at Holmes is the one in Miss Silverton's belly," says Charmaine, my big sister third from the top.

"That's segregated. And the Supreme Court has said it's time for black and white to blend."

I don't see why. It's not like we're going to rub off on them.

"Where is this new school?"

"In the Hollywood Hills," Mama says.

Hollywood Hills sounds like I'm going to be a movie star. I check myself in the shine of the toaster. Look like a young Sidney Poitier. Start practicing my autograph on the plate.

"How's he going to get there?" Lenai, the oldest, asks. "We don't have a car." She's the practical one. Parent Number Three, we call her, behind her back.

"He won a spot on the bus."

Two slices of toast pop up like eyebrows. Two eyebrows —mine—pop up like the crusts on that toast. How can I win what I didn't even try for? Then Daddy says they tried for me. Signed me up for a new program.

"Opportunity Busing, it's called. You got the last spot."

"I see," I say. "And what time in the morning will my alarm clock have the opportunity to ring?"

"Five thirty. Bus comes at six fifteen."

All five of my big sisters bust up. Lenai, who hardly ever smiles, is laughing. Cecily the Dreamer, always lost in the drawings she does, looks up from her sketchbook, laughing. Charmaine, boy crazy and bull stubborn, is laughing. Nika and Ebony, identical twins born a year before me, who like to fool the world as to who is who, are laughing. All five of them are laughing. Laughing at me.

Last year I got to sleep till seven. They know I need my beauty rest.

"What's the name of this school?" I ask.

"Wonderland."

"*Wonderland?* You're sending me to a school called *Wonderland?*"

"What difference does it make what it's called?" Daddy says in a tone like a loaded gun.

"It's the difference," I say, "between a boy who gets jumped and one who gets left alone. Can you see me stepping off that bus at the end of the day? Kids around here be all, *Yo, Armstrong, we hear you're going to a new school. That's right. What's it called? Wonderland. Wonderland? Say, Alice, what's it like down that hole?*"

"That's exactly why we're sending you. To get away from ignorance like that."

"Well, I'm not going," I say, arms locked across my chest. You got to be firm with people. Especially parents.

Blam! Daddy's fist comes down hard on the table. That's my cue to jump up and run. I've got the advantage when I'm on my feet 'cause he left the one leg in Korea.

"Armstrong, sit down on this chair!"

Daddy picks up the chair, slams it to the floor. *Crack.*

"Ain't no chair now, Daddy. It's a three-legged stool."

"*Isn't a* chair. And that's nothing some wood glue and a clamp can't fix."

I squat on that three-legged stool like I'm in a public toilet afraid to make contact with the seat. Start praying for this to be a short talk.

"Did Rosa Parks give up her seat on the bus?"

"No, sir."

"Then why are you so quick to give up yours?"

There he goes again, bringing up some hero of black history. Every time I sass him, he throws back a legend in my face. How am I supposed to grow up brave like Jackie Robinson, wise like Thurgood Marshall, or strong like Mohammad Ali when they're all looking down at me from Daddy's high shelf?

My legs wobble and burn. I can only catch every third word.

Courage . . . country . . . pride.

In the shine of the toaster, the future movie star starts to sweat.

Change . . . chance . . . pushups.

Pushups?

"No, sir, no pushups for me. I heard everything you said."

"Then you'll go to Wonderland?"

"Yes, sir. I will follow the White Rabbit down the hole."

"Good. Now hop along and do your chores."

I should've run while I had the chance.

Charlie

The leading cause of death for kids between ten and fourteen is unintentional injuries. Freak accidents like getting hit by a car, riding your bike off a cliff, or sticking a fork in a light socket. With statistics like those, why am I sitting in a tree?

Andy called it our Thinking Tree. Its botanical name is acacia, which is what Dad called its twin that blew over once in a storm.

"Boys," he said, firing up his chain saw, "I'm going to need a little help bundling up the acacia." Andy and I had been playing Battleship on his bedroom floor. We looked out the window and saw this massive tree lying in the yard. It had fallen all the way to the front door. "I'll cut up the branches. You bundle and drag them to the curb." Dad tossed Andy a ball of twine. "And remember, boys, do a man's job."

We were boys and men in one breath. Andy put on his ski mask, goggles, parka, and gloves. I wore shorts and a tennis shirt. By nighttime I was squirting Bactine over my arms and legs, Andy was wheezing from an allergy attack, and Mom was combing tiny green bugs from our hair. Tree bugs, we called them. The next morning I found one up my nose.

From the fifth branch of my Thinking Tree, I can see the streetlight by our house. It hasn't come on yet, so I'll sit here and watch until it does. Any time you see the streetlight come on, Andy always said, you're guaranteed good luck the next day.

I wonder why all my friends are changing schools. Do their parents know something mine don't, like we're getting a new principal who'll double the homework and cut the field trips in half? Have all the good teachers gotten better jobs someplace else? Or is there a toxic substance leaking into the water supply, and all the kids who stay at Wonderland will die from accidental poisoning?

Last year in the United States, more than six hundred kids died from accidental poisoning.

Dad's Vespa comes rumbling home from the Mulholland Tennis Club. He's been spending most of his free time up there, playing tennis or gin rummy with his friends. On weekends especially, he'll finish breakfast and say, "Well, I'm going up to the Club." And he vanishes on the Vespa.

The garage door wheezes up. He backs the Vespa into its slot, then steps onto the driveway.

Everything about my dad makes a big sound. He's got Paul Bunyan feet that rattle the walls when he comes downstairs. When he chews a sandwich, you can hear the lettuce crunch. Even his keys sound like heavy chains.

"Hey there, Dad," I call down from my branch.

"Charlie," he says, looking up at the tree.

Some kids have dads who are dictionaries. Mine's all twenty-two volumes of the World Book Encyclopedia in one brain. Whenever there's something I need to know, I look it up in my dad.

"How come nobody's going to Wonderland this year?"

"You're going to Wonderland this year."

"Most of my friends aren't. Keith's mom says it's going downhill."

"Your mother and I don't think it's going downhill. It's taking a different path. Some new kids are coming."

"From where?"

"A housing development in South Central LA. It's ninety-nine percent black."

The opposite of Laurel Canyon, which is ninety-nine percent white. Not boring white. We've still got hippies living in the Canyon. Rock stars too, like Graham Nash, Joni Mitchell, and Carole King, whose daughter was in Andy's class. And we've got movie producers like Reggie Jones, who lives across the street and throws wild parties with naked ladies in his pool.

Can you blame a boy for peeking?

We don't have many black people, though. There were a couple of half-black kids at Wonderland last year, but that family moved out of the Canyon. The only all-black people I know, besides Mrs. Gaines the Yard Supervisor, are Nathaniel and Gwynne, who work for my dad.

"Don't they have their own schools?" I say.

The streetlight is taking a long time to come on.

"The Supreme Court has ruled it isn't fair to keep black and white kids separate. Our city is trying to bring them together by busing some up here."

"Are they busing any to Carpenter?"

"Carpenter seems to have missed the map."

"So that's why so many families are sending their kids to other schools," I say. "They're racist."

"I wouldn't go that far, Charlie. They're doing what they think is right for their children."

I can't help it. Just for a second, my eyes leave the streetlight to look at Dad's face.

"And you and Mom?"

"We're doing what we think is right for ours."

I look back at the streetlight. Just my luck: it's already on.

Armstrong

As the only boy in a house full of girls with a working mama and a one-legged daddy, guess who gets all the nasty chores.

When my daddy's drips land on the bathroom floor, I get the blame—and the sponge. When the toilet clogs with whatever it is females put down there, who do you think is given the honor to plunge? And the one time we had mouse droppings in the bathroom, did they call an exterminator?

No. They called me, Armstrong Le Rois.

You ever empty out a mousetrap? Most people take the longest shovel they can lift, scoop up the dead mouse—trap and all—and chuck it into a brown bag, then throw the bag away.

I wasn't allowed that luxury.

"Mousetrap costs forty-nine cents," my daddy said. "When's the last time you earned forty-nine cents?"

So instead I had to peel back the metal bar and shake the dead mouse into a grocery bag so I could reuse the trap. It was nasty and I didn't want to do it.

"Can't somebody else empty the trap?" I said.

"Who you expect that to be?"

"I've got five sisters."

"They're too squeamish."

"Mama, then?"

"She sees enough death at the hospital."

"Why not you?"

"I saw enough in Korea. You don't want The Flashbacks to come, do you?"

The Flashbacks are my daddy's nightmares that come by day. He can be in the kitchen making dinner or paying the bills when all of a sudden he starts to scream like a thing in the forest, calling out names of men I never met, shouting words I'm not even allowed to whisper.

When I was little and The Flashbacks would come, I thought they were ghosts in the house. I'd hide under the table and grab hold of my daddy's one leg like it was a tree that could save me from a flood. He'd scream and I'd shake. He'd yell and I'd pray—for The Flashbacks not to touch me with their damp, cold hands.

Soon as the nightmares stopped, my daddy would reach down and lift me into his lap.

"It's just The Flashbacks, Armstrong. I never know when they're going to come."

"Can I help you fight 'em?" I'd say.

"You just did."

Another chore I've got is to help my sisters fold the laundry. It's something we all do together because six kids times their clothes is a lot of clothes. Since tomorrow's the first day of school, everybody wants to start with a clean pile.

Here's a pretty little tank top Charmaine wore all summer. I fold it up and put it on her stack.

Daddy plucks it off.

"That's Charmaine's," I say.

"It's yours now."

He puts it on top of my jeans. A pretty little *pink* tank top.

"I'm not wearing that. It's pink."

"What's wrong with pink?"

"Girl's color."

My sisters all bust up again.

"Armstrong, do your sisters take sewing?"

"No."

"Do they take cooking?"

"No."

"What *do* they take?"

"Shop class with the boys."

"And why's that?"

"'Cause you marched into the school and said your girls can do anything a boy can." *Except empty out mousetraps,* I think but don't say.

"And my boy can do anything a girl can, right?"

"*Most* anything," I say, hoping he won't ask for the exceptions.

"Including," Daddy goes on, "wear a pink shirt. Now, this one cost three ninety-nine. When's the last time you earned three ninety-nine?"

But Charmaine's not ready to hand down the tank top. She plucks it off my pile and puts it back on hers.

"I like the way it fits," she says.

"So will the eighth grade boys," says Daddy, putting the tank top back on my pile. Then he reaches over to Cecily's, nabs a top two sizes up, and drops it onto Charmaine's.

"That's my lucky shirt!" Cecily says.

Daddy takes another shirt—this time off Lenai's stack —and puts it on Cecily's.

"What am I supposed to have," Lenai says, "one of Mama's? One of yours?"

"You can have a new one. That's how hand-me-downs work. The oldest gets a new shirt."

And the youngest gets a pink one.

Charlie

Mom has spent the last hundred days mostly in bed. She gets up for important things, like the bathroom or morning coffee. Some days she gets up to shower, and some nights she comes down for dinner, which Lily cooks. Once a week, Lily drags her to the market.

Lily is our housekeeper. She came to America in the trunk of a car and had to pay a *coyote*, or smuggler, to get her here. Her room smells like Olvera Street, where she goes on her days off because Olvera Street reminds her of home. Dad's the only one who really talks to Lily — he took Spanish in high school. Sometimes I listen in when she's on the phone with her family in Guatemala or watching TV. But to me, Spanish sounds like Jiffy Pop.

Mom used to tuck me in at night. Now I tuck her in. The bed smells like perfume plus coffee mixed with today's *Los Angeles Times*. A headline peeks up from under the covers: "Ford Pardons Nixon."

"Tomorrow's the first day of school," I say.

Mom's face crinkles up like she forgot.

"Do you have everything you need?"

Good time to ask. Bullock's closed an hour ago.

"Dad took me shopping. I got new jeans. Went up a size."

She smiles her rubber-band smile. It stretches, but it doesn't curl.

There's nothing worse than losing a child. That's what all the people said when they crowded into our house for a whole week last May. They came with pink bakery boxes and cold cuts from Art's Deli. They all had more or less the same thing to say.

We can't imagine what you're going through.

A parent's worst nightmare.

Buzzer words, I call them. If life were a game show, a buzzer would go off every time someone said them.

If there's anything Eleanor and I can do.

Bzzz.

Thank God you still have Charlie.

Bzzz.

You could sue, you know.

Triple *bzzz.*

There's nothing worse than losing a child.

It must be true. She hasn't said Andy's name since he died.

"Good night, Mom."

"Good night, honey."

She hasn't said mine, either.